Epilogue:
The Dark Duet

CJ Roberts

Copyright © 2013 CJ Roberts, Neurotica Books, LLC
www.aboutcjroberts.com

Createspace
ISBN-13: 978-1484816066
ISBN-10: 1484816064

Photo credit: Yuri Arcurs

Cover design: Amanda Simpson
www.facebook.com/pixelmischiefdesign

Edited by: Emily Turner
Email: dpemily@gmail.com

Printed in the United States of America.

Books and Stories by CJ Roberts
Captive in the Dark (The Dark Duet, Book 1)
Seduced in the Dark (The Dark Duet, Book 2)
Epilogue (The Dark Duet, Book 3)

Stories by Jennifer Roberts
High Stakes Nikki (Sexy Shorts)
Manwich (Sexy Shorts)
Seducing Sunshine (Sexy Shorts)

**Books with contributions from
Jennifer Roberts**
Sin City: Six Scintillating Stories (Anthology)
High Stakes Nikki
Some Like it Bi (Anthology)
Seducing Sunshine

For Caleb's Kittens
And their Tomcat

There was only one thing the void wanted. Greedily tearing me apart, it asked for Livvie. It wanted my hopes, my dreams. It wanted my memories of her face. It wanted the laughter we had shared. "Mine," the void had decreed. Only Livvie could make me whole, and as soon as I had realized it, I couldn't stop looking for her. --
Caleb

CHAPTER ONE

I'm writing this because you begged. You know how I love the begging. In fact, you probably know too many things and know them far too well.

It's been a long time since *Captive in the Dark*; today is Friday, February 8th, 2013. In May it will have been four years since I sat in a tinted sedan and contemplated kidnapping Livvie. I'm twenty-nine now and I finally know it for a fact. Sometimes I wish I didn't because I have to face turning thirty in August. Livvie is eight years my junior, but you wouldn't know it by the way she talks to me sometimes (I think she just likes getting a spanking). Livvie and I have changed considerably from the people you read about. However, because you begged so nicely, I will endeavor to tell you the story you want to hear.

Before I move on, a word about names. They were very important in Livvie's books and it's worth mentioning. Shakespeare asked, "What is in a name?" I can tell you—a whole hell of a lot.

Livvie is now named Sophia. She changed her name when she entered the witness protection program in the United States in exchange for her testimony against her kidnapper and rapist (that's me).

However, you know her as Livvie and so I'll continue to call her that for your benefit, but of course, that would beg the question: Who am I?

Am I Caleb?

Am I James?

I've often asked myself this very thing and have always come up with a different answer. Perhaps the only truthful answer is, "I am both."

Caleb will always be a part of me—probably the largest part. I want to be James.

James is a 29-year-old from Oregon. He was raised by his mother and always wondered about his father. He grew up with respect for women but also a need to display his masculinity to make up for his lack of a father. He went to college but took time off before grad school to go and see the world. He met Sophia at *The Paseo de Colon* and fell instantly in love.

James never met anyone named Livvie. He never hurt her.

We know different. We know the truth. So, for the purposes of this story you begged me to tell—I am Caleb.

I am the man who kidnapped Livvie. I am the man who held her in a dark room for weeks. I'm the one who tied her to a bedpost and beat her. I'm the one who nearly sold her into sexual slavery. But, most importantly, I am the man she loves.

She loves me. It's quite sick, isn't it?

Of course, there's more to our story than can be surmised in a few short sentences, but I'm at a loss for justifying my behavior back then. I assume if you're reading this, I don't need to make those justifications. You've already made your own.

You're reading this because you want to know about the rest of the story. You want to know what happened that warm summer night in September of 2010, the night I met Livvie at *The Paseo*. It was the night my life changed all over again.

It didn't happen exactly as Livvie said. She's been very kind to me in the retelling of our story. The truth is far more... complicated.

Livvie would have you believe we kissed and it was all that needed to be said.

I wish it had been so simple. The part about the kiss is true. She kissed me. It had been a year since we touched. A year since I'd watched her walk away. An entire year since she killed for me and I repaid her by dropping her off at the Mexican border covered in blood. She kissed me and my head *did* swim. I can tell you unabashedly, it was probably the happiest I'd ever been before.

Then she slapped me. Hard. I think my head vibrated.

I remember holding my face together and thinking, "I'm going to jail now."

"How could you?" Livvie asked. I could hear the pain in her voice and it gutted me.

I believed she'd moved on. She'd made a life and I'd come along one last time to fuck it up. It was the minute that would never end. In that single minute, I replayed Livvie's and my time together in my mind and I berated myself for ever thinking she could forgive me for the things I'd done.

"I won't run, Livvie. I'll let them take me and you'll never see me again." I couldn't meet her eyes. I'd been dreaming of her for so long, imagining her face smiling at me. I couldn't bear seeing her disgust toward me. I didn't want to remember her that way.

Slowly, the longest minute of my life ticked away. I couldn't hear any sirens; there weren't any men slamming me to the ground and putting me in handcuffs. It was strange.

"Never see you again? How stupid could you be? You can't just walk into my life and expect to leave me again. I won't let you, Caleb. Not this time."

And if you can believe it... she slapped me *again*.

"What the hell is wrong with you? Stop hitting me!" Livvie was a blur. She hit me so hard my damn eyes were watering (I was *not* crying—eyes water. I think we all know I'm a badass and I don't cry). After I cleared my eyes, I could see the anger in hers, the hurt... but also her longing. She longed for me. I knew it only because I could recognize her face as a mirror of my own.

"How could you leave me, Caleb? I thought... I thought you were dead," she cried. She wrapped her arms around my waist and held me tight. It felt so good to have her in my arms again, I couldn't think of anything but the feel of her against me.

"I'm sorry, Livvie. I'm so sorry," I whispered into her hair. I couldn't believe I was with her again. I can't even describe it to you. Suffice to say, if I'd died in that moment, I'd have been fine with it.

We stood there for a long time. She held on to me. I held on to her. We said things with our silence we couldn't put into words. I suppose that's what she meant by, "it was all that needed to be said."

I felt all the things I could only have felt with Livvie: hollow, and simultaneously, full to bursting.

"I've missed you, Livvie. I've missed you like you wouldn't believe."

I don't know how long we stood there holding one another as tourists passed us by. We were simply another couple, enjoying the warm evening together. No one knew who we were or what we had been through to get to that moment. However, even in that elegantly prolonged circumstance, I knew it couldn't last forever. I had many things to say to Livvie. I was afraid of the things she might have to say to me.

I felt her shaking in my arms, her shoulders quaking against my chest, and I knew she was crying. I didn't hold it against her. She was more than entitled to her tears. I, unfortunately, couldn't express myself in quite the same way. So much had happened to me in my life. I'd cried all the tears I had in me to weep. All I could offer was strength. I could be strong for her. I could hold her, rock her, and shield her from the dozens of eyes around us.

The women glared at me as they passed. "What did you do?" their eyes accused.

The men sent pitying glances or condescending smirks my way. "Sucks to be you."

I ignored them. They weren't worth my attention.

"Can I get us out of here?" I asked. I felt the gentle nod of Livvie's head against my chest. I pulled back slowly, not sure if I was prepared for what might happen next. Suddenly, it didn't matter. Livvie looked up at me, and even with tears in her eyes, she smiled. I had been waiting a long time to see her smile. It had been worth every horrible second I'd been without her.

"I missed you too. So much," she whispered and wiped her eyes. "I'm sorry, I didn't mean to cry. It's just... it's so fucking good to see you!"

And then *I* smiled. I took her hand and we walked. All around me, life seemed surreal. I'd have thought I was in a dream were it not for the way my face stung. I was tempted to mention it, to make a joke of some kind to break up the tension just under the surface of our joy, but I opted to say nothing. Livvie was with me and it was all that mattered to me.

5

"Did you drive?" she asked.

"I did," I replied somewhat awkwardly. "It was optimistic, I guess. I figured either it would be my last opportunity to drive the streets of Barcelona, or I'd be driving you back to my place in style." I laughed half-heartedly. The longer it took to get to my car, the more awkward the situation became.

Livvie stopped walking and I jerked to a halt.

"I don't think I'm ready for that... Caleb." She looked around as if making sure we weren't alone. She slipped her hand from mine.

I tried not to let it bother me. Of course she'd be frightened to go anywhere with me, but it still stung. I tried to smile as sincerely as possible and shoved my hands in my pockets.

"We don't have to go to my place. I'll take you anywhere you want to go. I just... shit, I don't even know what I'm trying to say."

Livvie gave me a weak smile, the kind that didn't reach her eyes. She looked so beautiful, and so sad. She looked just as I remembered.

"I don't know what's wrong with me. I've been a wreck for the last four hours, just dying to get here so I could see you and now..." She crossed her arms around her stomach and lifted one hand to pull at her bottom lip. It was one of those gestures she made unconsciously and I remembered it well. It reminded me that no matter how much she'd changed in the last year, there were things about her that would never change.

It was only natural for her to wonder about the ways I hadn't changed. Frankly, it took every ounce of my self-control not to grab her and abscond. I had come so close to having everything I wanted, and in a split second it seemed things between Livvie and me would end before we even got to the car.

I suddenly didn't trust myself.

"Maybe... this was a mistake?" I edged. I wanted to give her the choice, but I wasn't sure I could bear to hear the answer.

She closed her eyes and squeezed herself a little tighter. Her brows knit together in what I interpreted as sorrow. Her head shook slightly from side to side.

I took it as a good sign. Her tells weren't choice—they were instinct. It thrilled me to know her instinct was to deny any possibility that meeting me was a mistake.

"I know what I want, Livvie. I want to be a part of your life again. I know we can't start over. I know you have every reason in the world to want me dead, but I—"

She placed her hand over my mouth.

"Don't. I'm not ready for that either," she said. She almost seemed angry with me.

I can never overstate the depth and beauty of Livvie's eyes. I can stare into them forever, until I forget my own name (which, let's face it—wouldn't take me long).

I took my left hand out of my pocket and covered her hand over my mouth. I kissed her fingers and nodded. It was as close to supplication as I could come without making a groveling ass of myself. It wasn't pride—it was stratagem. If I had thought groveling would get Livvie into my car, I would have made a good show of it. I'm shameless.

Slowly, Livvie pulled her hand away from my mouth and curled her fingers around mine. She shook her head and smiled ruefully.

"I don't know what I'm doing either, Caleb. I've wanted this for so long. I've put certain aspects of my life on hold, thinking—hoping that one day you'd find me again. And now you're here and I have to be honest… it's freaking me out."

I stepped closer to her. I was elated when she didn't take a step back. Her hand was warm in mine and her red lips were simply begging to be kissed again. She'd caught me off guard with the first one. I was desperate to make the second kiss last.

"I know. I don't expect you to trust me, but, Livvie, I would never do anything to hurt you again. Just give me a chance to prove it. How can I prove it to you?" I couldn't resist the urge to stroke her bronzed shoulder. She looked like a goddess. She looked like sex on silky legs. Her kitten tongue, just like I remembered it, swept her bottom lip as she pondered her response. "You're killing me with that, Livvie."

Her head tilted to one side.

"Killing you with what?"

I took a chance and tugged her a little closer. I removed my other hand from my pocket and let my thumb run across the curved bow of her lips. We swallowed.

"I want to kiss you again, but I'm afraid I'll scare you away." I took a step back when she tensed. "So I won't."

It was almost more than I cared to take. The impulsive man in me that was used to getting what he wanted at any cost was tempted to take control.

I realize you've somehow been lulled into believing my baser urges had been overcome, but that couldn't have been further from the truth at the time. I had spent the year prior to our reunion righting old wrongs, and sometimes it had meant being the man Rafiq had raised me to be.

"How did you find me, Caleb?" Livvie's voice was small and her fear irritated me because I knew she had a right to it. She cared about me. She wouldn't have shown up if she didn't, but I hated her trepidation just the same. "What do you want me to say? You know who I am. You know what I do." I let go of her hand before she had a chance to pull away from me again. The night was quickly going to shit. I was glad she didn't have me arrested, but I hadn't really planned for a scenario involving lust and incredible awkwardness.

"Hey," she whispered. "I don't mean it like that. I'm happy to see you, I am! But if you found me... what makes you think someone else can't?"

I felt like an idiot.

"It wasn't easy. If it weren't for our conversations, the things I know about you, I don't think I would have found you. You're safe, Livvie. No one's coming for you. I swear it." I didn't mention that I'd killed anyone who would have bothered.

"What things?" she asked. I could hear the hesitation in her voice.

"Do you really want to know, Livvie? Because once you know, I can't take it back." I let my eyes meet hers. I was willing to do a lot of things to win her, but she had to accept the harsh truth that I wasn't a man who played by society's rules and I never would be.

"Did you hurt anyone?" Her eyes implored me to say no.

"No," I said honestly. I even managed a flirtatious smile. She smiled back.

"Then I guess I don't need to know." She reached for my hand and tugged me in the direction we had been walking.

"This still doesn't solve the problem of what we're going to do when we get to my car."

"Is it a stick shift?"

"Of course. Why? Did you finally learn to drive?" I laughed at the memory of her admitting she couldn't drive. I laughed even harder when she scowled at me and playfully hit my shoulder.

"Asshole."

"Aww, you like it when I tease you."

"No. I don't."

"Then why are you smiling?" I whispered the words in her ear as we walked. All became right in my world when I felt her nudge me with her shoulder and her hand held mine a little tighter. The void in me sighed. I had found a way to feed it.

"I can drive. I'm not good with a stick though."

"I don't remember you being quite so bad with mine." A smile played across her lips as she gawked at me. If there's one thing I know how to do, it's flirt.

"I've seen you handle your stick, Caleb. You're much better at it than I am." She kept eye contact with me as I stared at her in shock, but she still blushed something furious.

I tried to make words come out of my mouth. I settled for smiling and shaking my head. She'd made me uncomfortable in the best way. It was a skill only she seemed to possess. I know it sounds juvenile, but there it is.

Finally, we reached my car. I'd be lying if I told you I didn't expect Livvie to be impressed. If you've ever stood in the presence of a Lamborghini Gallardo Superleggera and not gotten a tingly sensation in your naughty bits, you have to be very young, very old, or completely fucking blind.

"Nice car," she said.

I could tell she was trying to be nonchalant. She didn't do it well. I knew what she looked like when her pussy was wet.

"Wait until you get inside. It's my favorite part." And yes, gentle readers, I am that fucking smooth. I didn't open the door for her, but considering I was used to women opening them for me, let's call it progress.

I slid against the soft black leather and reached for Livvie's safety harness. Within the enclosed space of the vehicle, her scent infiltrated my senses. I took my time pulling the straps across Livvie's chest. I could feel her anxiety like a physical caress, but I didn't think it had to do with fear.

I was mere inches from her red lips. They were gently parted. I could hear her taking soft open-mouthed breaths. I looked up into her eyes and noticed immediately how they seemed both vigilant, and heavy with desire. She was watching my every move very carefully.

I leaned closer to her. I moved slowly, giving her every opportunity to say no or push me away. Carefully, I braced myself against her door with one hand. I didn't want my weight against her, not yet. I brushed the end of her nose with mine, urging her head to tilt upward. I felt her breath against my mouth, faster and heavier than before. And at last, I watched her eyes close as she leaned forward.

I let the tip of my tongue trace her bottom lip, coaxing her mouth open. I didn't want to rush things. Well, I did want to, but I know when I shouldn't. I wanted to push her up against the door, rip off her panties, and ram myself into her, but I suspected she wouldn't appreciate it as much as I would. It was enough to feel her lips opening for me. I came a little closer and she let out a soft whimper into my mouth.

She wanted me. She wanted me as much as I wanted her.

I kissed her for a long time. I couldn't get enough of her moans. I liked to threaten to pull away and let her lean forward, chasing after my mouth. I was pretty sure if I used my skills in the right way, I could get Livvie into my bed. I could see every glorious inch of her. Taste her pussy in my mouth before I wrapped her legs around me and fucked her until there was no come left inside me.

I heard myself moan, but I didn't give a fuck. I hadn't had sex in months, and the sex I'd had since Livvie wasn't worth mentioning or even thinking about. I'd jerked off before I came to meet her and my balls still felt heavy. I took a chance and removed my hand from the door. I let myself caress her shoulder to gauge her reaction to my touch.

"Caleb," she sighed. She gripped the edges of her seat and pushed her chest out slightly. Her tongue pushed harder and deeper into my mouth.

Fuck! Yes! I wanted to yell the words. I reached for her breast and my cock throbbed when I felt how hard her nipple was against my palm. I could tell she wasn't wearing a bra beneath her dress and the thin fabric let me feel every contour of her. As quickly as I could, I pushed on the harness and released the straps. I pulled the fabric aside and Livvie's beautiful breast came into view.

"Caleb!" It wasn't a sigh this time. She was a little panicked.

I didn't let it stop me. I could still hear the lust in her voice. I palmed her breast and put my mouth around her puckered nipple. I sucked on her greedily. I moaned loud and gripped her harder when her cry hit the air and her hands held on to my head, pulling me closer.

Somewhere in my lust-addled head I knew the situation wasn't ideal. As sexy as a Gallardo Superleggera is, it's incredibly cramped and certainly wasn't conducive to the all-out fuck-fest I had in mind. It took every ounce of self-control I didn't possess to pull myself away from Livvie's delicious nipple.

It was harder not to go back to it when I got a good look at Livvie upon pulling away. Her body was tilted at an angle, with her head against the door, and her dress was pushed to the side to expose one of her breasts. Her nipple was hard and wet from my mouth. Livvie's lipstick deserved an award because it had surprisingly stayed on her lips and wasn't smeared all over her face.

"Let me take you home, Livvie. Please. I can't stand being this close to you and not being inside you for one more fucking second." I put myself out there. I let her know exactly what my intentions were.

She was slow to catch her breath. Her dark brown eyes looked on me with lust, but also with what seemed to be a myriad of other emotions.

"What's wrong? I know you want this as much as I do." I tried not to sound annoyed, but it's next to impossible not to sound like an asshole when my dick is hard enough to pound nails and I'm expected to have higher brain function.

Livvie eyed me warily. Sadly, it was an expression I'd come to know very well in our time together. She could probably tell I was annoyed and it was scaring her. Carefully, she set about adjusting her dress and slipping her breast back into it. She couldn't seem to stop fidgeting, and with every movement it became obvious she was pondering her next actions.

Then, with her gorgeous tits no longer in view and her racy dress smoothed down to reflect a more demure appearance, she spoke.

"I want to ask you a few questions, Caleb, and I need for you to be completely honest with me. Can you do that?" She looked toward me with her sad brown eyes.

She had me in a precarious position and I was willing to do whatever it would take to make her happy again. I wanted the opportunity to taste Livvie's happy tears again.

"Ask me anything you really want to know. But only if you think you can handle the answer." I couldn't stress my point enough. She couldn't ask me for honesty and then hate me for following the rules. Well, she *could*—but it's a shitty thing to do to a person.

"Okay," she said resolutely. "You drive and I'll ask my questions."

I raised a disbelieving brow.

"Wouldn't it be easier to ask me now, when I don't have to navigate in traffic? And where exactly do you want me to take you?"

Livvie smiled coyly and it made my chest ache. She could be such a tease sometimes.

"I want you distracted, Caleb. I don't want to give you the chance to shape your version of the truth. You're far too good at half-truths. Just drive around and I'll tell you when to stop. Stay in the city—no rural roads." She reached for her harness and strapped herself in.

I didn't know if I was offended or impressed, but I decided to go with the more agreeable of the two.

"Don't trust me?" I asked and smiled. She'd always been a fan of my smile.

"To a point," she replied smoothly. "I trust you enough to get in your car, but you can't blame me for being cautious."

I could feel my face and neck getting hot. I wasn't immune to my guilt. I felt guilty for a lot of things where Livvie was concerned and she was right. She was entitled to much more than caution. I cleared my throat to break through the tension. I adjusted myself as surreptitiously as possible, put on my harness, and started the car.

"Whoa!" Livvie gripped the door handle as the car roared to life and the engine caused our seats to vibrate.

I smiled at the knowledge her pussy had received a little tickle. My balls appreciated the RPM too. I pulled away from my parking spot and tried to concentrate on navigating our way out of the tourist-filled traffic. In the pit of my stomach, my anxiety churned and threatened to ruin my dinner.

"Okay, I'm all yours. Ask me anything you're prepared to have answered." From the corner of my eye I could see a smile tugging at the corners of Livvie's mouth.

"You're all mine?" she asked.

I looked in her direction.

"Are you serious? That's your first question? This might be easier than I thought. Yes, Livvie, I'm all yours." I winked at her for good measure. My stomach felt a little better when I saw her smile.

"And you're mine, only mine." The void fed on the memory.

"Good to know. But it won't be that easy. When you offered to take me home, did you mean my house?" Her tone hinted at her unease.

I suddenly knew where this conversation was going to go. However, I'd promised to answer her honestly. I always kept my promises. All, except one. I pushed the thought away.

"You didn't want to go to mine, so I thought yours might be better."

"Do you know where I live?" she accused.

I rolled my eyes.

"Yes."

She was quiet for a while, but I couldn't really gauge her thoughts because I had to focus on the narrow, disjointed streets.

"Okay," she said resolutely. "It makes sense you'd know where I live. I'm sure it took you a while to find me."

"It did." I smiled again, but I can't be sure it was genuine. I don't like answering questions, especially ones that sound like a trap.

"How long have you known where I am?" The tone of her voice was less than friendly.

"Livvie, I—"

"Caleb. You promised."

I gritted my teeth.

"I've known for a few weeks." I slammed on my brakes to avoid hitting a group of drunken idiots crossing the street. Fucking teenagers, they thought they owned the world. I rolled down my window without thinking and yelled at them. "Get the fuck out of the road!" One of them gave me the finger and called me a fag in Spanish. "I'll show you a fag, you little bitch. I'll fuck-start your head!"

"Caleb!" Livvie cried out and gripped my arm. I snapped my head toward her and I could see she was more than a little frightened. It irritated me more than I understood at the time. I watched as the group of soccer idiots kept walking down the street. They were still laughing and shouting at me. I wanted to shoot each of them in the kneecaps.

A horn blared behind me. I stepped on the gas and propelled us into a roundabout a bit too quickly.

"This isn't going the way I hoped, Livvie. You're obviously scared of me and I'm just getting irritated. Maybe I should take you home." I felt a pang in my chest as I spoke. I didn't want to take her home, at least not to drop her off. But I couldn't take much more cat and mouse. It's just not who I am.

"If that's what you want, then I think you better." She was definitely angry.

"No. It's not what I want. I wouldn't have gone through all the damn trouble to find you if that's what I wanted. Please be rational."

"You be rational, Caleb. You show up out of the fucking blue and just expect me to fall on my back and throw my legs open for you? No! Not until I know what the hell you've been up to for the last year. Not until I know why you're back in my life and what you expect from me."

Okay, that made sense. I knew it did. I didn't have to like it. My entire life had changed. I'd given up everything I knew and the last thing I wanted to do was talk about it. Why do women have to do so much talking? If you're hungry, eat. If you're thirsty, drink. If you want somebody to fuck the guts out of you, just say so!

Of course, I knew I couldn't say any of those things without proverbially shooting myself in the foot. I'd come to grovel. I'd fucking grovel. I took a deep breath and slowed down. The car could practically idle and do 40kph.

"I don't expect you to fall on your back and throw your legs open." I spoke calmly. "But it would be nice." I glanced in her direction and gave her my most suggestive smile. She glared at me.

"I don't know what I expected, Pet. I've been thinking about you for a long time. I guess I just want to say I'm sorry. I know I can't erase our past. I can't promise you I'm a completely different person. I'm messed up in ways most people can't possibly understand, but I care about you. I had to find you and tell you you're the only thing I care about anymore." I kept my eyes on the road and swallowed hard. My pride is thick and I may have had to swallow more than once to force it down.

She sighed.

"I... care about you too, Caleb. The past year hasn't been easy for me. It's not just moving, or letting go of my family and friends...." She was silent for a minute. When she spoke, there were tears in her voice. "You betrayed me."

She may as well have slapped me again. Maybe punched me in the stomach for good measure. She knew how much the word "betrayed" would get to me.

"How?" I asked the question as smoothly as I could.

"I was ready to go with you. After everything you'd done. And you just... left me. You have no idea what I had to go through. How hard I had to work to become... *human*." She whispered the words. She looked out the window and watched the same streets pass her.

I'm not sure where I went mentally. I kept circling the same large block. I remembered that day. I had replayed it in my mind a million times in the past year. What could I say to her? The truth was awful. I'd killed Rafiq the day before. I'd buried the only family I had ever known, and I was reeling with the discovery he had been the cause of every horrible thing that had happened to me. I loved him. I killed him. I couldn't look at Livvie without comparing myself to Rafiq. I had kidnapped her, tortured her, raped her, and taken her away from everything she knew. And she said she loved me. That had been the worst part.

"I wanted you to be sure." My words sounded alien, wooden. I felt Livvie's hand on my arm. It startled me

18

and brought me back from the place I'd been. I took a few seconds to just look at her. She was so damn beautiful—not only on the outside, but on the inside as well. She was stronger than me. She was braver. She didn't want vengeance.

"I know why you made me get out. It took me a long time to accept it, but I understand. I know it was your way of being selfless, your way of sacrificing. But you made me sacrifice too. I almost went bat-shit crazy." She smiled genuinely and I couldn't help but follow suit.

"You are crazy, Livvie. But I wouldn't have you any other way." I turned my hand over and she moved her hand into mine. It's stupid how happy it made me. "In case you haven't noticed, I am not the poster child for mental health."

"Oh, I noticed."

"Bitch." I feigned insult.

"Asshole."

"I missed you," I said.

She squeezed my hand.

"Take me to a hotel, Caleb."

I visibly straightened. There was a fleeting moment of internal struggle while I contemplated giving her answers to questions she didn't ask, but in the end I just had to be me. I am the master of half-truths.

"I know just the place."

CHAPTER TWO

I wasn't sure what to expect when I put the keycard into the door. I knew what the room would look like. I knew Livvie would think it was beautiful. I knew there was an enormous bed waiting to be soiled. What I didn't know was if I'd get the chance to use it the way I wished.

"Wow, Caleb." Livvie stepped inside and put her purse on the coffee table. "You certainly know how to make an impression. First the car, now the room."

I shrugged from the foyer.

"The car's rented. Technically, so is the room. I have good taste though; no one can deny me that."

"No, I guess they can't." She wandered to the curtains and pulled them back. It seemed to be a clear indication she didn't trust me.

I took the insult as best I could. How insulted did I really have a right to be? I knew she believed the hotel to be a secure place to meet. All she'd have to do was scream and someone would probably hear us. Of course, the key word there was *probably*. I was tempted to remind her that if I were so inclined, she wouldn't even get to scream. However, I figured it wasn't in my best interest to point such things out to her.

I walked into the living area and made myself comfortable on the sofa. I wanted to get the preliminaries out of the way as soon as possible and get back to more pleasurable pursuits. In the meantime, I watched Livvie. Always inquisitive, my Livvie, a curious little kitten. I eyed her from my seat as she ran her long fingers along the furniture, the drapes, and the Tiffany lamp on the desk.

"Livvie." She focused on me. Her nerves were obvious. "Come sit with me."

She shook her head slightly.

"I'm not sure that's such a good idea."

I rested my head on my fist. I stared. On this point there would be no discussion. I'd made my request clear and I expected her to acquiesce. I wasn't going to argue moot points. I took great pleasure in exerting my dominance. It was fun watching her squirm.

Taking my bait, Livvie filled the silence.

"Caleb... come on. You know the second I go over there you're just going to pounce on me." She was biting her lip again, her fingers nervously tugging on it. "Caleb? Are you even going to say anything? Oh, okay, so you're just going to sit over there, looking all 'you know you want me'? I'm not scared of you, Caleb." She crossed her arms over her chest and tried her best to look intimidating. "I have pepper spray in my purse!"

I couldn't help it. I burst into laughter.

"Oh my god, you're such a jerk," she said. She walked toward me and unceremoniously plopped onto the sofa. "Fine! I'm here."

I was still holding my stomach when my laughter finally subsided and I could make eye contact without starting up again.

"I'm sorry, Livvie, I really am. You kill me. Pepper spray? I've tracked you all over the world and that's what's going to stop me—pepper spray."

Livvie's wide grin was my reward for all the slaps and insults she'd thrown my way during the course of the evening.

"Well, maybe it wouldn't stop you. It would still be fun to watch you roll around on the ground crying for a while." She shrugged. "It might still be fun."

We laughed for little while, diffusing all the tension. I felt completely at ease by the time we were done laughing and I knew Livvie did too. Her shoulders had dropped. Her fingers had stopped fidgeting.

"I missed you, Caleb."

"I missed *you*, Livvie."

Livvie took off her heels and set them beside the sofa. As she pressed her toes into the carpet and grabbed at the thick fibers, she smiled at me. She sat up straight, bending her knees so she could sit on her feet. It was a relaxed and casual pose. It was a good sign for things to come.

"All over the world, eh? Tell me about that."

I stared at her for a second, but I relented. It was best to get it out of the way. I took off my shoes and adopted a more comfortable pose as well. There is nothing more unattractive than having to stop getting naked to remove one's shoes. I like to think ahead.

"Yes. I looked for you everywhere and anywhere I could think of. If you really wanted me to find you, you could have left me a note in Mexico. It was the first place I looked." I reached out with my right hand and stroked Livvie's cheek. I loved that she let me.

"I didn't think it was a good idea. The FBI knew you'd left me the money. I was afraid if I left you a note they'd know you were alive. I couldn't risk it." She smiled, though it didn't quite reach her eyes.

I felt many things upon hearing her words. I was touched. I was angry. I was sad.

"I'm sorry you had to go through that. They made you change your name." I hadn't counted on Livvie. I'd been too sick about Rafiq to believe she'd ever try to protect me.

"I like my new one." She reached for my hand and held it on her knee. "I'd do it again, Caleb—in a heartbeat. I don't know how you feel about it, but I want you to know I'm happy. I have a great life."

"I guess that counts for something. If I'd let you come with me... I don't know. I doubt you'd be the same person. I doubt you'd be as happy as you seem to be." My own words gave me pause. I'd been right to leave her behind. Had I been right to return?

She gave me a sidelong look. Her smirk hinted at amusement, but her eyes promised retribution.

"You're not off the hook, Caleb. If you hadn't left me at the border with a gun, I wouldn't have had to make a scene to get back into the country. They were barely even looking for me. So don't give me that 'all's well that ends well' bullshit."

She got a chuckle out of me.

"Point taken. So how was your time with the FBI?" I was genuinely interested in what she had to say. I'd had some close calls in the past year. At the time, I assumed it was the FIA in Pakistan trying to find me. I was sure they didn't appreciate Rafiq had gone missing, nor the fact he had been connected to the *Zahra Bay'*. I played with my life every time I went into the country. I wondered if the FBI had been looking for me too.

Livvie looked sad for a fleeting moment before she plastered a smile on her face.

"I'll get to that. There's a lot you should know. First, I want to know how you found me. I want to know what you've been up to. I don't want to have to change my name again."

"What happened to doing it again in a heartbeat?" I provoked.

"Don't be an idiot," she said and nudged me with her knee. I let out a defeated sigh.

"After Mexico, I decided to try your old neighborhood." Livvie looked aghast. I was quick to reassure her no one had been hurt. "I didn't talk to anyone. I couldn't take the chance. I waited outside your former apartment building, but I realized pretty quickly your family didn't live there anymore." I inched a bit closer to Livvie on the sofa. I didn't move so much she'd notice—at least not right away. "I must have scouted the bus stop for weeks, just hoping. Which, in retrospect, was pretty dumb. Why would you go back there?

"After your old neighborhood proved fruitless, I remember you talked about your friend Nicole. And before you get all huffy—I didn't talk to her either. I just stole her laptop."

"Caleb!" Livvie admonished.

I shrugged unapologetically.

"Are you glad I found you or what? Your whereabouts weren't just going to fall out of thin air." I practically dared her to tell me there had been another way. "I found an email that could only have come from you." I moved a tiny bit closer. I don't think she realized. "You sounded really sad. You mentioned going to the Eiffel Tower by yourself. Someone stole your wallet. It was months after the incident, but I still worried for you. You said you weren't over me."

Livvie looked away from me. She had tears in her eyes and she was working hard to make it seem as though she didn't. While I didn't necessarily relish her pain at the memory, it boded well for me. It made me believe there was a chance for us.

She cleared her throat and wiped at her eyes with the back of her finger.

"Ugh! I thought I was past this part. I promise I'm not quite as emotional as I used to be." She smiled. "I guess you just bring it out of me. I like your hair. How long is it?"

"It's camouflage. I keep it back because it annoys me when it touches my shoulders." I didn't want to talk about my hair. I reached up and collected a tear racing down her cheek. I drank it. I knew it didn't make sense to her. If anything, she seemed more embarrassed. However, it was my way of taking her pain away. It was a promise. I didn't go around drinking random tears. I'm not *that* creepy.

Livvie took a deep breath and exhaled slowly. Some of the tension from earlier was slinking its way back into our intimate moment.

"Some things never change I guess," she whispered.

I moved closer, until our knees brushed. My arm rested on the back of the sofa and I was able to touch her hair with my fingers. Warmth spread through me as I watched her eyelids slide shut.

"Everything is in the process of becoming something else. It's the law of change." I briefly kissed Livvie's eyelids before she could open them. "I'm in the process of becoming something else, Livvie. I hope it's something good, something far removed from the monster you knew."

"Wow!" Livvie said. Her tears had gotten the better of her and she raced to put distance between us. She wiped hurriedly at her cheeks. "Holy shit, Caleb. How can I keep from being a mess when you say things like that? I don't even know how to feel."

I smiled and moved back. I had her where I wanted her, but more than that—I had her where I *needed* her. In a place where she could admit she could forgive me for the past. In a place where *we* were possible.

Over the next several hours, I relayed the many airline tickets I had purchased to search for her. The places I had almost caught up and missed her. I told her about Germany and the café. She hadn't been happy to hear about that one but accepted I wasn't quite ready to approach her at the time.

She attempted to ask questions about our last days in Mexico. I was honest and told her it was too much for me to discuss so soon. I'd tell her at some point. She didn't like it, but she used it as leverage to dodge questions about the FBI and what she'd learned about me.

For the most part we tried not to delve too deeply into subjects that were excruciating to either one of us. It was more about discovering how we felt toward one another after so much time had gone by. As our feelings became more obvious, we were able to discuss our present instead of our past. I liked that much better. I liked hearing about Livvie going to school. I listened to her talk about the endless possibilities of her future and it made me feel somewhat better about... well, everything. I would be lying if I told you I was over what happened with Rafiq—far from it. Still, it gave me a modicum of solace to know that if he had lived, Livvie's future would not be so bright.

Too quickly, the hours had ticked by. The night had gone silent and in a few hours, pre-dawn would be approaching. My thoughts began to turn toward more carnal diversions and talking had begun to lose its appeal.

"It's late," she whispered. She had her feet on the sofa, her knees pulled up to her chin. Her dark eyes begged me to come closer. Her legs threatened to push me away.

I felt myself getting hard, my dick throbbing in rhythm with my heartbeat. I was transported to Felipe's plantation in Madera. I remembered the first night I whipped her. She'd known she was in trouble and she hid under the sink. She was curled up in much the same way, eyes staring up at me, legs trembling ever so slightly. I remembered the thrill of making her surrender.

The memory filled me with mixed emotions. I had been her abuser. I had taken something from her she had been unwilling to give. I felt guilty. Yet, I also had a fondness for the memory. It had been the beginning of my exploration with Livvie. Even cowered beneath the sink, her eyes had met mine. She fought me without words. She fought my possession. It was in those moments I first saw the ghost of the boy I had been. I knew the words behind her stare: You can have my body, but you can't have me.

I had admired her even as I was resolved to bend her to my will. She had closed her eyes at our first touch, gathering her courage.

"Look at me. I want you to look at me."

In the quiet hotel room, with Livvie only a short span away, I stared into her unflinching eyes and once again read the message. I wouldn't be able to take what I wanted this time. This time, I had to earn her surrender.

"I don't want this night to end," I said. I wanted to make myself as clear as possible. Whatever she decided to do after that was fine.

"So… what then?" She raised her hand to her mouth and tugged gently at her lip. Her eyes had a mischievous glint.

"Well, the way I see it, you have three options: You can make me very sad by asking me to drive you home. You can take pity on me and spend the night. Or you can admit you want me to fuck you until you beg for mercy." I leaned back and put my arms around the sofa. I let her see how hard I was for her, how much I wanted to be inside her.

She inhaled sharply. Her cheeks reddened. A quick glance downward revealed her toes, curled tightly.

"You... still have a way with words." Her voice was breathy, but confident.

"Just laying it out for you." I winked at her. I felt pretty confident about which of the three options she would choose. However, she has a way of throwing in her own surprises.

"I still have the pepper spray," she teased.

"Kinky." We laughed.

I knew she wanted me. It was written all over her face. It was in the way she licked her lips in preparation for being kissed, the way her eyes seemed to go dark. I had a moment of hesitation. I wasn't sure what role she wanted me to play. On the one hand, it would have given me pleasure to tell her what to do. I liked being in control. I liked knowing she'd obey me of her own free will. On the other, I wasn't sure how my dominance would be accepted. The last thing I wanted to do was scare her away. I didn't want to remind her there had been a time she hadn't had a choice.

"So, what's it going to be, Pet?"

She raised a brow.

"Pet?" She didn't seem put off by the moniker, despite the gentle warning in her tone.

"Force of habit," I whispered unapologetically. *Slow and easy it is.*

"You have a lot of bad habits, Caleb."

"But not all my habits are bad, are they?" I let my hand rest on my dick. Her eyes followed my movements. She swallowed.

"No. There's a few I'm quite fond of." She met my eyes and held me captive.

"Do tell," I suggested.

"Give me time, Caleb. I will. But... tonight? I just need you to know I'm not the scared girl you remember."

She brought her knees down and opened her legs. Her dress hid what was beneath, but her message was clear as she placed her hand on her pussy.

My heart beat erratically, spurred by her seduction. Beneath my own hand, my cock strained against my zipper.

"I remember you were brave," I managed to say beyond the lust clogging my throat.

"I remember you liked to watch me touch myself." She inched her dress up her thighs. Her short, blunt fingernails left faint red trails along her smooth tan skin. "I remember I liked watching you too." She shifted down and rested her head on the arm of the sofa.

I was beside myself. My mouth was dry—too many open-mouthed breaths. My chest felt bruised by the incessant pounding of my heart. Lower down, my flesh was rigid and surrendering its first clear droplets of seed.

"I'd like to do a hell of a lot more than watch." I leaned forward and was met with instant resistance. Livvie's foot pushed against my chest and urged me back against the sofa.

"We do it my way. Or not at all," she threatened playfully.

I knew a battle I couldn't win when I encountered it. I tilted my head toward Livvie in deference.

"I can accept that." I resumed my previous posture. "I await your every whim." I baited her with my smile.

"Good." She relaxed. Her fingers trailed lightly over her pussy. "You show me yours... and I'll show you mine."

I laughed softly. If it were possible to care for her any more, I wasn't sure I could stand it.

"Hmm," I sighed and unzipped my jeans. "As I recall, shyness was *your* obstacle, not mine." I quickly undid my pants and opened them. My lust intensified as my cock hit the air. I resisted the urge to touch it. I took great satisfaction in hearing Livvie gasp. To her credit, she composed herself quickly.

"Very nice, Caleb. I know we're both in the process of becoming something else, but it's nice to know there are a few things that will never change." She lifted her knee closest to the couch. Her dress rode up toward her waist. She spread her legs and revealed her naked pussy. She hadn't been wearing any underwear!

I reached for my dick and squeezed it. I wasn't in any danger of embarrassing myself; the impulse was simply too much to ignore. I took a deep breath and let it out slowly. I stroked myself once, twice, and stilled my hand.

"You're fucking beautiful."

She blushed.

"Thank you. So are you."

I wasn't sure how I felt about being called beautiful, but I took the compliment. I had much more interesting things on my mind.

"What now? I have to be honest; I'm not sure I can sit here and watch you play with yourself. I don't have the self-control."

"Would you force me?" she whispered. Her fingers parted her pussy, revealing how pink and wet she was.

"Fuck! No. But I'd be really childish about it." I stuck out my bottom lip and she laughed.

"Oh my god," she said through a smile. "You're making this really difficult. Don't ruin my fantasy."

I composed my face.

"I'm sorry. Go on. Far be it from me to deny you another fantasy. I was so fond of the last one." I watched her mouth and remembered the way her lips slid over my cock. "Maybe we could relive that one too?"

"Maybe," she teased. "If I come over there, will you put your arms on the couch and keep them there?"

I swallowed.

"I'll try." I raised my arms to the back of the sofa and gripped it. I'm hard again just remembering how sexily she crawled across the sofa toward me. Livvie is a predator in her own right.

My eyes drifted shut at the first touch of her hand against my chest. I knew she could feel how hard my heart was beating. I might have been more nervous than she was. Her dress was soft as it caressed my aching cock.

"Your dress is going to get ruined. Take it off," I whispered as enticingly as I was able.

"Shh," she whispered against my ear. The smell of her skin infiltrated my senses. I held tighter to the sofa. "I want it just like this." Her thighs straddled mine and her wet pussy made contact with my dick. I thrust upward. I couldn't help it.

"Goddamn it, Kitten! Just let me fuck you already." I was ready to abandon all chivalry and self-control. I was ready to rip her damn clothes off and bury myself so deep she'd forget we were ever separate people. The only thing that stopped me was the sudden pain of Livvie pulling on the tie holding my hair back. Once free, she buried her hands in my hair. She pulled my head back and the pain refocused my attention. Her eyes were nearly black, her pupils wide with desire. She was enjoying herself. I didn't want to stop her.

She placed soft kisses against my mouth as she spoke.

"Please, Caleb. Let me. You're still in control." Her hips moved against me. Her pussy was hot against my cock. "You're bigger, stronger. I know that. It turns me on that you'd let me do this to you. You'd never let me before."

I held tight to that damn sofa because I suddenly knew why it was so important for her to have the upper hand between us. This encounter was not about earning her surrender—it was about surrendering myself. She was testing me and I refused to fail.

"Okay, Livvie." I panted against her mouth. "We'll do it your way." Her tongue invaded my mouth and we kissed.

"You can call me Kitten if you want to. I miss it," she crooned. She didn't give me a chance to respond before her tongue was in my mouth again. There was no protest when I rocked against her.

Finally, she seemed to have enough of her own teasing. She leaned back quickly and reached behind her neck to undo the buttons. Accomplished quickly, her ample breasts, complete with pebbled nipples came into view. I licked my lips as I stared at them.

"Give me," I insisted.

With her hands on my shoulders, she raised herself up onto her knees. My dick felt cold without her heat. Only the promise of her breasts in my face was enough to quell my disappointment. Livvie is soft, ridiculously soft, and the flesh of her breasts against my face was a feeling just this side of heaven. I placed kisses on one and then the other, ignoring her non-verbal cues for my mouth on her nipples. I could be a damn tease too!

"Caleb!" she said with some irritation. I smiled.

"Yes, Kitten?"

"Please." She held her breast and ran her nipple across my mouth. "Suck on me."

I opened my mouth and pulled her into it. She tasted even better than she smelled. I sucked harder than I probably should have, too driven by my lust to stop. Livvie's arms wrapped around my head, forcing me closer, not

32

letting me move away—though I had no intention of it. I softened my suckling. I let my tongue flick at her nipple, slowly and repeatedly. I made her insist on more. Livvie was slow and maddeningly calculated in her seduction of me. Though she writhed against my chest, all but begging me to take control, she let me know I wasn't to move my arms away from their resting place. She fed me one breast and then the other. She liked watching me, she reminded. For as much as we both wanted things to be different, our history could never be erased. I knew she was punishing me for the things I'd done. As far as punishments went, I knew I was getting off too easy.

Pulling away slowly, she slid her body down my chest and put her head on my shoulder. She moaned once she made contact with my cock again. I just managed to keep my body from responding. I was ready. I was *more* than ready. I wanted to touch her. It was beginning to feel unreasonable that I couldn't.

"I'm nervous," she whispered against my neck.

"Don't be. All you have to do is tell me I can touch you." I was close to doing it anyway.

"No. I'm still mad at you." She laughed softly.

"Someone once told me you shouldn't let vendettas run your life."

"She probably never had you like this." She lifted her head and watched me. "If she knew revenge could be as sweet as this, she'd never stop seeking it out." I smiled.

"Let's hope not."

I lost all logical thought as I felt Livvie's hand travel down my chest toward her spread thighs and my cock. I let my head fall back when I felt her tentative fingers wrap around my flesh and guide me toward her pussy. She was so hot, so wet, and the pressure required to get the tip inside her hinted at how tight she would be.

"Livvie," I said insistently. "Please let me touch you." Her soft lips kissed my throat.

"Tell me again how much you missed me." Her hips rocked back and forth, trying to accommodate more of me. She whimpered but wouldn't admit her difficulty.

I lifted my head and looked at her. Her face was a mixture of pleasure and pain, yet her eyes remained determined. I swallowed thickly.

"I missed you every day, Kitten. Every. Fucking. Day." I raised my hips and felt myself slide into her a little deeper.

"Oh! God!" She pitched forward and held on to me. "Caleb," she sighed. She was panting already. "Take it easy. I haven't done this in a while."

Her words brought me up short. I found myself suddenly jealous and angry. I was reluctant to show it. I didn't have a right to my anger, except it didn't matter—it was there. I stopped moving.

Livvie gained her breath and slowly rocked against me again. I tried to ignore the pleasure it brought me to gain further entrance into her body. She smiled at me and I scowled.

"Don't be mad, Caleb." She slid up a little on my dick and let her bodyweight push me deeper on the way down. I couldn't stop the moan that escaped me. "I meant you. Not since you."

My chest seemed to expand and contract in unison. It was barbaric, selfish, and nevertheless, I didn't give a shit. Livvie belonged to me. Yes, I'd been with other women since her. In my heart, they had counted for nothing. I broke my promise, but still surrendered. I surrendered to Livvie's power over me. I surrendered to the havoc she unleashed on my control. I raised one of my hands and pulled Livvie's face toward mine. I needed to be inside of her. I needed my tongue in her mouth and my cock in her body like I needed my next breath.

We moaned into one another's mouths as our bodies instinctively moved against each other. I moved my other arm off the sofa and wrapped it around Livvie's waist. I had her pinned against me. A dark thrill rushed through me as I yielded to my primal nature to conquer.

I stopped kissing her and held her still as I bent my knees and thrust into her. I heard her cry out, but she didn't ask me to stop. Her arms wrapped tightly around my head. I thrust again, and again, until at last, I felt the whole of me inside her tight heat.

I felt incapable of speech. I had wanted her for so long. I had dreamt of her in my sleeping hours and ached for her in my waking ones. There was nothing I could say to compare with the intense elation and satisfaction of finally having that which I had desired for so very long. Nothing except—

"I love you."

I didn't intend to say the words. I knew she wasn't ready to hear them. However, I'd been waiting to tell her since the moment I watched her leave and I couldn't hold it in a minute longer.

Livvie burst into tears and held me tighter to her chest to keep from meeting my eyes.

"Don't stop," she sobbed. She moved her body, sliding herself up and down my cock in a rhythm that demanded I keep pace. I was at a loss for what to do. It seemed I'd done and said enough already, so I did the only thing I could: I did as I was told.

Pressed so close to Livvie's chest, it was easy to find my way to her breasts again. I put my mouth around one of her nipples and resumed my previous attentions. I palmed her ass in both hands. I was rewarded with moans and sighs instead of sobs. All the while, I felt her pussy trying to accommodate me further. Her wetness came more freely after a moment. Her muscles relaxed. I could move faster, push harder, and go deep on every forward thrust. The sound of my balls making contact with her wet flesh, her moans above me, the heat and tightness surrounding me—it all spurred me toward my crisis.

"More, Caleb. Oh, god, please!" Her words were a high-pitched plea. Her movements were frantic and disjointed. She was chasing an orgasm that wouldn't come and then came too hard and fast.

I fucked her through her climax. Her pussy contracted around me, her muscles were rigid, and her sounds begged me to slow down. I couldn't. I kept pounding into her until her orgasm subsided and she collapsed limply against me.

"Please, Caleb," she panted against my ear. Her breasts were sweaty and they slid against my chest. Beneath my sweater, I was caked in sweat too. I wasn't going to stop to take it off. "Slow down." I knew she had to be tender, especially after she'd come so hard. I forced myself to slow. "Yes," she sighed contentedly, "I like that. Fuck me just like that."

"Stop saying fuck," I panted. "Or I won't be able to slow down."

She giggled.

"I'm sorry. You bring it out of me." She found her way to my lips and kissed me. After a while, her movements fell into rhythm with mine. She pushed down as I thrust up. She pulled away when I did, only to meet me with equal force.

"God, you feel good," I murmured against her mouth. I delighted in her mewling whimper and increase in pace. I hadn't forgotten her silent rejection. Truth be told, it stung like a motherfucker, but I knew it wasn't the time to bring it up. I'd made that mistake already.

"Fuck me," she said though harsh breaths.

"Beg me," I demanded. Two could very well play this game.

"Please, Caleb." She held my face in her hands and looked into my eyes. If I had found my primal nature, Livvie had also found hers. Her need was unmistakable. Her lust intoxicating. "Please fuck me with your huge fucking cock. I want to watch you come." She slid her eyes shut and moved her body harder and faster.

She certainly knew how to push my buttons. I only hoped she wouldn't regret it. I held her with one arm as I raised us off the sofa and pushed her onto her back. I finally reached for my sweater and pulled it off. I pushed my jeans down to my knees while I was as it. There was a moment of resistance on her part that quickly evaporated as I pushed myself in to the hilt.

"Again, Kitten. Beg me." Braced on one arm and holding her outer thigh, I watched myself fuck her. Remembered words made me smile. She was just right shade of pink. I glanced up and watched her breasts moving to the rhythm of my thrusts.

"Please, Caleb."

I couldn't hold back any longer, but I wasn't sure I should come inside her.

"Where do you want me to come?"

Livvie's eyes pierced me with their intensity.

"Wherever you want."

It hit me before I had a chance to decide. My balls drew up tight and I started coming. I tried to watch Livvie, but my eyes couldn't stay open. I was lost to the feeling of being emptied, of being received into Livvie's body.

Somewhere outside myself I knew Livvie was speaking. I couldn't hear her clearly until my orgasm slowly subsided. I opened my eyes and looked down. Her hand was between us, touching the place we were joined.

"Mine," I heard her say. Nothing had ever been truer.

"Yours," I said.

CHAPTER THREE

I dreamt that night.

Rafiq looked up at me from a table. He was shaking from fear. His face was bruised and bloody. He spoke calmly.

"Me for the girl?"

A ripple of love was fast on the heels of my shame. The feeling was quickly overrun by an old anger, a rage that had kept me alive when death had been a far better option.

"No. Not just for the girl. You... made me love you. You betrayed me."

Rafiq laughed, loud and rich, before his laughter devolved into gurgling coughs.

"Betrayal again. It's always betrayal with you, *Khoya*." His words sounded in my mind as though he were flesh and blood again. "You lie, boy. I didn't make you love me. One cannot force love. What you gave, I earned."

I held a knife in my hand; I knew I did. However, as is the nature of dreams, it disappeared once I tried to plunge it into his thigh. I had so much anger, so much rage, and nowhere to put it. Rafiq found it more than amusing and it only fueled my hatred.

"I gave you all you earned when I put a bullet in your heart!"

Rafiq coughed up blood as he laughed.

"You are the man I raised." Slowly, his laughter subsided and he looked on me fondly. "I know you washed my body. I know you buried me in accordance with the law. I know you wept for me."

His words wounded me despite knowing there was no way for him to know I did those things. Worse, it hurt knowing they were true.

"Why won't you die?" I asked with venom. Rafiq smiled wickedly.

"You can't kill me, *Khoya*. Not again. I'm all you know. I am your mother. I am your father. I am your brother. I am your friend. I'll always be here. You'll never be rid of me."

As much as I loathed it, I was free to weep in my dreams and I did.

"How could you have done all those things to me? You stole my childhood. You stole my destiny."

Rafiq, suddenly unfettered, rolled onto his side and sat up. The bruises on his face had healed and clothing had magically appeared on his body.

"That's not what's bothering you, Caleb. I betrayed you, yes, but that's not why you killed me, is it?" I couldn't look at him while I processed my shame. "You would have killed me anyway. You would have killed me because it's the only way I would have let the girl go. *You* would have betrayed *me*, *Khoya*. We are not so different, and that's what eats at you." He raised a hand and ruffled my hair as he used to when I was young. My chest ached.

I pushed him with all my strength, knocking him backward over the table and onto the floor. I leapt into the air and landed on top of him. I punched him. Repeatedly. My fists felt ineffectual; I couldn't get the force I required to beat him to death. Switching tactics, I held his neck in my hands and tried to squeeze the life out of him.

Rafiq's maniacal gaze fell on me.

"I am a god here! You've made it so."

"Just fucking die! Die! Die! I hate you! I wish you were alive so I could kill you all over again!" I dug my fingers into his eyes, growing hard as blood oozed onto my fingers. Rafiq tried to fight me this time. His hands pushed against me, his legs flailed, and his body twisted as he tried to buck me off. "I can kill you, Rafiq. You're not a god. I feel nothing for you."

Rafiq's body went still under me.

"Master?" I heard a voice behind me. I turned and saw Livvie. She was wearing a white robe that reached the floor. Her hair was loose and unruly. She wore a slave collar at her throat. A wave of overwhelming guilt slammed into me.

"Livvie? Don't look!" I turned my head toward Rafiq. His body had disappeared. Only a large bloody stain remained. My hands were covered in blood and gore. I wiped my hands on my thighs, but the blood wouldn't come clean. "Don't look," I said and I was sobbing again. "Don't look."

Livvie's footsteps approached and I could actually feel the weight of her arms wrapping around my shoulders. Her warmth descended on my back.

"It's okay, Master. I know why you do it. You can't help who you are." I hunched over and her weight followed me.

"Don't look."

There are moments that define our lives. At the time, most of mine were comprised of people I had murdered or enslaved. I'd done something about the slaves. I couldn't take back the murders. I didn't want to. However, my subconscious was not appeased by my belief in justifiable murder. I enjoyed it a little too much, my subconscious admonished. I was a little too "well-adjusted" for someone inured to such treachery.

I woke to find Livvie's body wrapped around me. Her chest was pressed to my back and her arm lay covetously against my chest. Her warm breath skated against my neck. I smiled to myself. So far, each moment with her seemed to be better than the last.

Panic lingered in my chest, but I had grown accustomed to the nightmares. I am nothing if not adaptable. What I found more frightening than the dream was the voice in my head telling me I'd never let Livvie go. *Mine. Mine forever.*

If you're sighing with contentment, you're either one sick fuck or you don't grasp the seriousness of the situation. While I no longer kill, I am a killer. A killer in love is a very dangerous thing.

I laughed softly because Livvie was spooning me.

"Mmm," she sighed. Her fingers caressed my chest. She pressed closer, her lips finding my neck and leaving a sleepy kiss. I reached for her arm and stroked it with my fingers.

"Are you awake?" I whispered. There was no way I was going to be able to go back to sleep. My dick was hard and Livvie was much too soft.

"No," she grumbled. I chuckled.

"If you're not awake, I can't have your pussy for breakfast." She twitched behind me. Her foot stroked my leg.

"Never stopped you before." She undulated against me.

"Oh?" I held her arm and rolled over. Her breasts felt hot against my naked chest. It went nicely with the silky feel of her thighs as I slid my cock against them. "Do you mind if I help myself then?" She bit her lip and tried not to smile. She was more than awake but determined to feign sleep. Her lipstick had faded, but red stain remained. Aside from the disorderly mess of her long hair, she looked every bit the goddess of the night before.

"Mmnmyeah," she muttered.

"You're fooling no one," I whispered against her neck. She didn't respond.

I pushed my own hair from my face. Livvie had been playing with it before we fell asleep and I hadn't bothered to tie it back up. It was annoying, but I traveled with a Swiss passport and it helped me look the part. I often traveled with a snowboard, though I had no idea how to use it.

I buried my face in her neck and inhaled. Her head fell to the other side, exposing her throat to me in clear invitation. Beneath me, her legs drifted open. The head of my cock missed the silk of her thighs but compromised by rubbing against the sheets. I'd get back to her heat soon—no rush. I took my time kissing the long line of Livvie's throat. She moaned and undulated against me. Her feet found the backs of my knees and rubbed.

"That feels good," she sighed.

"Shh, you're supposed to be asleep. I'm having my way with you." I used my thumb to trace her nipple until it was a hard little pebble.

"Well, could you take advantage of me a little faster?" Her arms wrapped around me and pulled me closer. Her intention to get me to suck on her nipples was obvious, but I ignored it. I'd already made reservations at a different restaurant.

"Don't make me gag you," I threatened. There was a non-verbal response from her, a slight tensing perhaps, but I was too otherwise engaged to think on it. I kissed and sucked my way down her chest and briefly stopped to tease her nipples with the tip of my tongue. I kept my pressure light. I didn't suck or lave. I wanted the air to do my teasing as I continued my way south.

Livvie's hands found their way into my hair and she grabbed handfuls of it. It hurt. I decided I might have to cut it if she was going to use it as makeshift handlebars. Then again, I couldn't blame her. I loved grabbing hold of her hair too. I decided payback would be more fun (and no one even had to die, which was a bonus).

Finally, I decided if she wanted me to pick up the pace, I would. I had waited too damn long already. I reached for her hands and disentangled her fingers from my hair.

"Let's put these somewhere a little less dangerous," I whispered against her taut belly. Holding one hand on either side of her hips, I pinned them there and shifted myself toward her pussy. I put my mouth on her without hesitation.

"Caleb!" she cried out. She pressed her feet into the mattress and pushed away from my mouth. I tugged her back down by her wrists and continued my assault on her clit.

I moaned against her. I loved the way she writhed on my face and I could already feel her getting slick. I traced her inner lips with my tongue. It wasn't long before she was using my grip on her wrists and her feet in the mattress to leverage herself closer. She wanted me to put my tongue inside her... and I would, when I was good and fucking ready. In the meantime, I enjoyed the smell and taste of her. Some men don't eat pussy. I think those men *are* pussies.

I sucked Livvie's clit into my mouth and licked her hard. I was rewarded with pain as she dug her fingernails into my wrists. She'd been pretty feisty since our reunion. I'd been slapped, teased, threatened with pepper spray, had my hair pulled, and then I was pretty sure she'd drawn blood. I didn't know what to make of it, but I decided I'd try fighting fire with fire. I squeezed her wrists until her fingers unfurled and she let out a whine.

I let her wrists go and sat back on my heels. Livvie's legs were wide open, her chest heaved with arousal, and her wet pussy begged to be fucked. It also didn't escape my notice that she hadn't moved her hands. I think that might have turned me on more than anything else.

"Flip over. Lift that sexy ass in the air." I swallowed past my arousal.

"Yes, Caleb." She rolled onto her stomach and adopted a posture I recognized immediately. I'd taught it to her.

I felt like someone had stroked my cock and punched me in the chest in chorus. Was it wrong to enjoy the view? Did she think I hadn't changed? Did she know I regretted ever forcing her to obey such commands? Why was I so damn turned on? Was I still the same man who got off on breaking her?

Not the time for ethical quandaries, asshole.

Shaking free of my thoughts, I placed one hand at the small of Livvie's back and held my dick with the other. I lined up my cock with her slick opening and thrust halfway inside her. I pulled back and thrust again. I didn't stop until my hips met her ass. Livvie cried out and fisted the sheets in her hands.

"God!"

I ran my hand up her spine, pressing her down. I jabbed her with my hips against her ass. They were short thrusts that had us both in a frenzy of lust. I leaned over and whispered in her ear.

"Do you like that?" She whimpered but didn't reply. It incensed me. I was reminded of a cheetah that had just spotted a bolting rabbit. I wrapped one arm under Livvie and grabbed a handful of tit. So close to her face, I reveled in every little gasp, moan, sigh, and whimper as I slammed myself against her harder. "I asked you a question. Do you like it?"

She bit her lip and her eyes squeezed shut. She had to be enjoying herself because I could practically hear and feel how wet she was. She refused to answer me. It was starting to mess with my head. The night before, I'd told her I loved her and she hadn't said a word. The pattern was disconcerting and I decided if she was trying to piss me off, it was working.

I lifted my weight off of her. I gripped her hips and slowed my rhythm. I looked down to watch myself sliding in and out of her. Indeed, she was sopping wet. Her shy little asshole beckoned. I smirked as I wondered if my next action would get her talking. I traced the puckered hole with my thumb. Her hips jerked, but then settled. I stepped it up a notch and let my thumb press its way inside her ass.

"What about that, Pet? Will that get you talking?"

"Mmm."

"That's it? That's all I get?" I became less angry. She liked it. She wanted me. She wanted the things I was doing to her. But for reasons yet unbeknownst to me, she couldn't come right out and say it. *Or maybe she's turned on pretending she doesn't.* I had to shake my head to make the thought go away. It was too much to think about right then. I pulled my thumb out and held on to Livvie's hips. I went at her hard until I felt her shake and shudder around my dick. I came inside her again and collapsed on the bed next to her.

"God, I am starving! I want breakfast so bad," Livvie murmured into the sheets. Her forehead was plastered with sweaty hair. I laughed.

"She speaks!" I pushed the hair off her forehead and she closed her eyes to enjoy my touch. What a strange pair we made.

"For a minute there I didn't know if I wanted to come or bolt out for pancakes." She smiled at me. "You certainly take it out of a girl."

"Hmm, I put some back in, too." I winked. "We have to check out of here in about fifteen minutes. We slept late." I knew it wasn't going to be a problem, but I still liked to give Livvie a hard time.

"Crap. That's hardly any time to take a shower and I only have the clothes from last night." She flipped over and huffed toward the ceiling. I rolled onto my side and propped up on my elbow.

"We could go to my flat. It's close."

"How close?"

I grinned. "Next door."

Her eyes got huge.

"You dick!" she laughed. "I thought you had a house."

"People say 'come to my house'. It doesn't mean they actually live in a house. I live in the hotel... but not in this room. You can't blame me for being cunning. *And*... we can order room service." I smiled broadly and waited for her reply.

Thank goodness for whatever hormones make women so agreeable after you've laid them right, because that's all it took to get her to agree. Also... pancakes.

CHAPTER FOUR

After our pancakes (and an obscene amount of syrup on some very interesting body parts), Livvie informed me she had to go to her apartment and get ready for work. I wasn't too happy about it, but I decided to be cordial and allow her some sense of normalcy. We'd had a lot of sex and done more talking than I cared for, but there were still plenty of things unresolved between us. I had my work cut out for me with Livvie. She wouldn't even let me take her home.

"I can take a cab home. I'll be in a rush when I get there and I'd feel bad ignoring you." She smiled at me while putting on her shoes. "Can I call you when I get off work? It'll be a little before midnight since it's a Monday."

I was still in bed, naked. I hoped my silent protest about putting on clothes after our shower would have inspired her to keep me company, but it didn't work. She still hadn't said anything about my confession. It was making me more nervous than I cared to admit.

"I still don't understand why you're leaving me. You know I'll get up to no good without you."

She smiled at me again and walked toward the bed. She bent down and kissed me on the cheek.

"I trust you." She moved away before I could drag her back into bed.

"You're not wearing any underwear," I teased. The last thing I wanted was for her to run into trouble with some cab driver.

"I think the odds of being kidnapped twice in a life-time are pretty slim. Don't you?" Her tone was meant to convey sarcasm, but there was an edge to her words that smacked of resentment.

I forced myself to smile when all I wanted to do was tell her I was through taking her shit. I knew I deserved it. I deserved much more than she was giving. It's just not in my nature to let people kick me while I'm already down.

"I suppose you're right. I'll be here if you call." I rolled out of bed, kissed her on the top of her head, and walked into the bathroom to take a leak. I heard the door shut.

I tried to keep my mind away from Livvie by keeping busy. I read a book. I returned the Lamborghini. I ate. I searched through local and international news. Regardless of my intentions, it wasn't long before my thoughts veered toward Livvie again.

I thought about the night before and her hasty exit in the morning. One set of thoughts made me smile; the other had me on high alert.

Livvie's apartment was near her school. I researched the campus and neighborhood. Crime was relatively low. The internet wasn't flush with stories of sexual assault at her college. However, I doubted the university would willingly offer such information. I made a mental note to investigate for myself at a later time. Livvie had a tendency to trust too easily.

I'd already done my due diligence and researched her neighbors. The man across the hall from Livvie had been arrested for domestic violence the year before but hadn't been in trouble since. He'd been living with a female student at the time. I'd be keeping a close eye on him as well.

I showered around ten-thirty.

I had champagne brought up an hour later.

By midnight, I was expecting the phone to ring at any moment.

With each passing minute, I realized the void inside me was alive and well. It was thriving. It had a taste for a new sort of misery—hope. It had been a long time since I had allowed myself such an emotion. The void feasted on it while old memories reminded me how dangerous it could be. Hope and fear are different sides of the same coin. I had gone from missing Livvie to hoping I could be the man she wanted. I didn't know which was worse.

I had gone through all sorts of scenarios in my mind prior to making contact with Livvie. However, her passive aggressive behavior toward me was not one of them. My mind is much more problem/solution oriented. Mad at me? Scream at me. Punch me if you're up for it. Please don't smile at me sweetly, act like nothing is wrong and then leave me disillusioned. And before you say anything, yes—I realize how fucking ironic my words are. I have played my fair share of mind games with Livvie. It doesn't mean I liked being on the other side. No man does.

I took a cab over to her apartment. There was a wall of buttons and a speaker panel just outside the door. I ran my finger down a column of buttons until someone buzzed me in. I ignored the groggy insults coming through the speaker. I made it a point to ignore the button marked "S. Cole."

The elevator to the fifth floor moved at a glacial pace. Thoughts raced through my mind, each bombarding me with different emotions. In the time it had taken to arrive on Livvie's floor, I had changed my mind about what to say or do a dozen times.

I could turn around, change hotels, and let her wonder where the hell I'd gone. I could pound on her door and make a scene in the hall. I could push my way past her when she opened the door and refuse to leave until she gave me answers. I could tell her to go fuck herself and then leave.

I could.

I wouldn't.

I took a deep breath and knocked. My heart beat a staccato rhythm and my breaths filled in the gaps. I'd been in more than my fair share of perilous situations, but few had the ability to affect me so physically.

After a few seconds, the door opened. A small chain prevented it from opening fully. Livvie's tear-stained face looked at me through the gap. My anger evaporated and fear blossomed.

"Are you okay? You didn't call."

Livvie glanced away and shut the door in my face. I heard her dealing with the chain just before the door reopened and she motioned me inside. I stepped slowly and carefully. As I let my eyes wander around her apartment, I realized I'd never walked in Livvie's world. I didn't know all the different sides of her. There was a blue sofa and a coffee table in the shape of a splat. Fake orange daisies stuck out of a vase filled with clear marbles. Framed posters adorned her walls: *Interview with a Vampire, The Crow, The Social Network, Inception*, a poster of four different colored records, and a half-naked man whose virtues were compared to chocolate.

I felt conspicuously out of place. Livvie was young. She cared about movies, music, and boys. She preferred bright colors. I smiled when I saw her PlayStation. A set of drumsticks, a microphone, and a plastic guitar were crammed up against the TV stand. I wondered if Livvie liked to sing or if she preferred one of the instruments. I wondered who she played with and decided the couple she was always with seemed the most likely. They knew her in ways I didn't. It made me jealous.

"I'm sorry," Livvie said as she walked toward a side door. She was wearing a pink robe with teddy bears on it. I would never have chosen an outfit like that for her. I followed her onto her balcony and watched her light a cigarette. "I got out of work late and I figured you were probably asleep." She inhaled deeply and let the smoke out smoothly, a sign of a well-seasoned smoker.

"How long have you been smoking?" I asked. I hadn't noticed her smoking during the course of my surveillance. She smiled and scoffed sarcastically.

"You going to give me shit about it?"

"No. We all have our bad habits." I would be doing something about the smoking, but I didn't need to get into it right then. She turned her head toward me and gave me a grin.

"Not all my habits are bad."

I smiled despite my unease.

"There's a few I'm quite fond of," I quoted her. I stepped closer and brushed her hair away from her forehead. I liked touching her. I liked to remind myself she was alive. To my relief, she closed her eyes and enjoyed my touch.

"I only do it when I'm stressed out. I took it up after I left the hospital. I haven't had one in months." She turned away and took another drag from her cigarette.

"What's the real reason you didn't call?" My fear surged. "Did you... change your mind? About us?"

She glanced at me over her shoulder before pointedly staring off into the night. She took two more drags from her cigarette.

"I don't know what us *is*."

My eyes were burning. The smoke, maybe.

"It could be whatever you want it to be, Livvie. Or it could be nothing. It's up to you." I knew the moment the words left my mouth they were a lie. She scowled at me.

"No, Caleb, it's not so simple. It's been a year. A fucking year! You never gave me the chance to be angry with you. You just disappeared and left me to worry that maybe you were dead. I had the FBI up my ass and the whole time—the whole time—I defended you. I defended what you did to me because I loved you and you'd just risked everything to save me. And now you walk back into my life." She wiped at the tears on her cheeks. "And goddammit I can't bear the thought of being without you again. But there's all this other shit too. All the things I never let myself feel because I didn't want to admit that maybe Reed and Sloan were right. Maybe I can't love you."

Adrenaline coursed through my veins as my dormant and underutilized emotions were accosted.

"Please," I heard myself whisper. I didn't even know what I was asking for. Perhaps it was only that I wanted her to stop saying those things. Her words hurt me. They hurt me more than I thought anything could hurt. They hurt nearly as much as the memory of Rafiq's eyes going dead. My own words taunted me.

"I did think it was really cute when you said you loved me though."

Livvie, in her infinite capacity for compassion, put out her cigarette and wrapped her arms around my waist. I took the lifeline she offered and held her in my arms. I might have squeezed her too hard. I didn't want to let her go. I couldn't.

"Caleb," she gasped. I loosened my grip but didn't let her go. "I don't want you to disappear again. Please, promise me you won't."

I searched blindly for my voice and had to clear my throat before I could speak.

"I promise, Livvie. But I... I don't know what to do. I've never been here before."

"Neither have I, Caleb. And we're seriously more fucked up than anyone else I know." She laughed morosely. "But you have to give me time. You have to let me be mad at you. You have to promise that no matter what I say or do, you'll forgive me. You'll wait for me to let it go."

So many emotions and I couldn't let them out. I settled for stating the obvious.

"Livvie, I'll forgive you whatever the hell you want. You don't need my forgiveness; you never have to ask for it. It's yours, Livvie. Anything that's mine to give is already yours." I placed my fingers in her hair and tilted her face up to mine. Her lips were salty with tears, her mouth tasted like smoke, but beyond that there was just Livvie. I needed Livvie.

In my best interpretation of every superhero movie I'd ever seen (and I hadn't seen too many by that time), I lifted Livvie into my arms and carried her inside. She kindly gave me directions to her bedroom. We made love on her pastel-yellow sheets amidst a ridiculous amount of throw pillows.

***

Later, after we'd finished having sex, Livvie engaged me in conversation. It reminded me of Mexico. We had always been better in the dark. I'm going to spare you and, admittedly, myself the agony of the details of what happened after we finished making love. You know what Livvie went through. You know the truth about my past. After that night, I knew it too.

I learned my name had been James Cole. I had been born to an American named Elizabeth Cole and a man known only as Vlad. I was five when I'd been kidnapped and sent to live as a whore. My mother killed herself when I was twelve. I couldn't help but take notice I'd been taken under Rafiq's care around the same time. I wondered if he'd known my mother was dead when he'd decided to "rescue" me.

I couldn't remember her face. I would always remember Rafiq's. Meanwhile a voice nagged me: Vladek is your father. Your father is still alive.

"Are you okay?" Livvie whispered against my neck. I could feel her tears dripping on me. I could feel her arm wrapped tightly around my chest. I could feel her heart beating against my ribs.

I felt. I fucking *felt* and it was awful.

I pulled her close and ran my fingers across the small of her back, taking whatever comfort I could find in having her close to me. She was alive. I was alive. We were together. I tried to focus on that.

"No, Kitten. I'm not okay," I whispered. "I don't know how long it's going to take for me to *be* okay. I just know that as long as you're with me, there's a chance that one day… I might be."

She squeezed me. So much was trapped inside me, and her love—or whatever it was she felt for me —threatened to coax it out. I fought to keep it all inside, where I could control it and no one could use it against me. My life was fucked up. It always had been. There was no point in dwelling on things I couldn't control or change. My mother was dead. Rafiq was dead. Livvie and I were alive. End of fucking pity party.

"I'm so sorry, Caleb," she sobbed. I closed my eyes to blink the burning and stinging away. "It wasn't your fault."

I swallowed hard.

"I wish that were true. Once, it may have been, but it stopped being true a long time ago. I did what I did, Livvie. It was my fault." We were quiet for a minute as the words settled. There was something I needed to know. "Livvie, why did you change your last name to Cole? Was it for James? Or... me?"

"Caleb, I know who you are. It doesn't matter what I call you as long as it's what you want." She sighed. "I did it because..." She shifted uncomfortably.

"You loved me." I closed my eyes. "Trust me—I didn't miss the past tense. I understand." I didn't understand.

"Caleb, it's not..." she whispered and pressed closer. "It's just... what you said about change. We're changing. We're both different, and until we know what that means, I don't think—"

"I don't want to talk about it, Livvie. I just want to be here. Right now. With you. Fuck the rest of it, because I don't care. If there's anything else you need to tell me, please do it now. Let's get it over with and tomorrow we can start over. I want to start over, Livvie. Can we do that?" I kept stroking her back. It kept me grounded.

"I'd like that. But what will we tell people? We can't tell them the truth, and I can't leave my life behind again, Caleb."

"What about the FBI? Are they still watching you?" I had a momentary flash of rage as I imagined coming face to face with Agent Reed. I'd pound his face into the ground—present tense!

"I'm supposed to meet Reed on Thursday. I know you don't like him. Hell, I'm not sure *I* like him." I could hear the smile in her voice and it irritated me. She'd compared him to me one too many times. "But he's a good guy. He wanted to check on me since I told him I felt like someone was watching me. Aside from him and Sloan, I don't deal with the FBI. I don't have anything they want." She nudged my ribs. I sighed.

"Well, you *didn't*. You do now. With any luck you'll be able to get rid of Reed easily. Tell him you have a secret admirer from school or something. I'm sure you do anyway. If you tell him there's nothing for him to look into, he'll be suspicious." A voice in my head asked me if I could get away with getting rid of him for good. I calmly ignored it. I was determined to be someone different. I didn't want to be a killer anymore.

"Okay, but what about the other stuff?"

"One day at a time, Livvie. I'm not ready to start explaining our relationship any more than you are. Let's take our time coming up with our story."

She propped herself on her elbow and leaned down to kiss my chest. She wiped at the wetness she had left on my shoulder.

"I swear I've done more crying in the past two days than I've done in the past year." She smiled. "I think I'm done now. I really didn't want to have to tell you all that stuff. It broke my damn heart when I had to hear it from Reed, but you deserve to know about your past." Her gaze traveled from my eyes to my chest. She stroked me casually with her fingers. "The way you looked that day… he wasn't worthy of your grief."

I placed my hand on top of hers and cleared my throat.

"It's over. I don't want to talk about it."

Her expression turned playfully wistful.

"If you'd have found me sooner, we could have celebrated your birthday. I lit a candle for you last month. I had to eat the cake myself." She smiled. Her words were strange to me, but I laughed too.

"What kind of cake?"

"German chocolate. It was soooo good," she groaned. I smiled, and at last it was truly genuine.

"Well, it's just as well. I don't eat a lot of cake."

"I do! Then again, I'm eight years younger than you and my metabolism can handle it. You have to watch your handsome figure." Her hand shifted down my chest and rubbed my abdomen.

"I think I do alright," I said. I wasn't shy about my body. I had no reason to be. "So weird to have a birthday, though. Do you think I look twenty-seven?"

Her smile was coquettish.

"I think you look... delicious!" Her hand traveled further down my abdomen until she brushed my cock with her fingers.

"Delicious, huh? That's a new one. I was thinking virile, or the male personification of perfection."

She laughed out loud. Her laugh was infectious. I loved the way it was a little too loud to be lady-like.

"Oh, Caleb. You're those things too. But right now? I'm more interested in your tastiness." She slid down on the bed and took my cock in her hand.

"Oh! Well in that case... taste away. If you have any more cake, I'd be happy to provide the frosting." She wrinkled her nose and I laughed.

I lay back and let Livvie blow more than my mind.

CHAPTER FIVE

Livvie's meeting with Reed went okay. He wasn't an idiot though, Livvie recounted to me. He wanted to hang around for a few days and make sure Livvie was safe. I didn't like him. I suspected his visit had more to do with uncovering secrets than keeping Livvie safe.

He spoke to Livvie's friends, her co-workers, even the kid at the restaurant Livvie liked to go to. It was a good thing I had paid someone to give my note to the waiter. If he'd given Reed my description, we would have been pretty screwed. It took a great amount of will power to steer clear of him. I knew there were certain things Livvie would not forgive.

Livvie and I had no contact during Reed's visit. I discovered more nightmares and a level of boredom I had never experienced before in my life. I was grateful for the internet until I was unable to resist doing a search for "Missing child+James Cole".

There were a couple of results, but nothing that jumped out at me. I was kidnapped before the internet had become commonplace, before Twitter and Facebook, and 24-hour news. Back then, milk cartons and mailers were the best people could do. James Cole never stood a chance.

That night I dreamt I was trapped inside a child's body. I was with Narweh again and my strength meant nothing. He laughed at me. I didn't go online for a week.

I never like it when I dream. It's usually about things I'd rather not think about. When I was a young boy and worked in the brothel, I never dreamed. At least, not that I can recall. There were mornings when I would wake and have new and interesting ways to murder Narweh when the time came—but I never attributed them to my dreams.

The first dreams I can recall began when Rafiq brought me to live with him. The uncertainty of my new fate had the tendency to terrify me. I have never felt comfortable sharing my feelings—especially my doubts, fears, hopes, and desires. They are what make me vulnerable and more than anything, I hate being vulnerable. Once Rafiq had gained my trust, once he had given me a destiny and a purpose, I didn't dream so much.

The dreams resurfaced in the weeks following Livvie's kidnapping. I had dismissed them at the time. I knew I was conflicted over many things: My desire to move on with my life. My confusion over Rafiq's increasing secrecy. The nagging sense of doubt over kidnapping Livvie. The fear I was becoming Narweh. The dreams intensified the more my feelings for Livvie had begun to develop. I denied it then. I see it now.

The nightmares I had after I left Livvie at the U.S.– Mexico border were some of the worst I have ever had. If you know anything about me—and we've well established you do—then you can perhaps imagine the horrors I had to choose from. The truth is, I don't let these things, the horrors of my past, drag me under. Quite the contrary— for so very long, they fueled me. Considering what I've been through, I often think I'm very well adjusted. I can handle anything the world throws at me, but for someone who tries to plan his moves ahead of time, uncertainty about my future leaves me disturbed as nothing else.

I thought finding Livvie would give me certainty, but I was learning that happiness also presents new ways to suffer. Misery, I understand. Happiness is terrifying.

Also, Livvie's words about "other shit" coming to the fore made sense to me. For the first time in my life I didn't have anything to do. No one had any expectations of me. I had enough money to do anything and go anywhere, but I had no idea what I wanted to do or where I wanted to go. I had idle hands. My mind was the proverbial devil's playground. It seemed as though everything I had kept tucked away in the dark recesses of my mind was escaping into my consciousness.

I breathed a deep sigh of relief when Reed left Spain and Livvie could finally come back to me. I still had the nightmares, but waking up to her warm body made it easier to come back from the anxiety.

***

It was October, and the weather was becoming unpredictable. On some nights it was the perfect excuse to spend hours in bed. Livvie and I fucked like rabbits—and a few other animals too.

Although Livvie's presence brought me solace after a nightmare, I hated how weak it made me feel to accept it. Instead, I took to staying up after Livvie went to sleep. I slept while she was out in the world of the living. I still had the dreams, but I didn't wake up to darkness.

All in all, things were good. Aside from the dreams, I didn't have anything to complain about. However, I'd be lying if I told you I wasn't beginning to get more than a little restless. Livvie had a job, she went to school and had friends. I didn't have any of those things. Trust me, I wasn't butt-hurt over it. I didn't begrudge her those things. It was simply becoming obvious to me that my life was completely different from what I had known. What does a former kidnapper/murderer do in retirement?

After three weeks of idle hands, I decided to buy a car. I bought a 5-Series BMW. It wasn't as sexy as the

Lamborghini, but it did the trick. I could go for long drives and avoid my sterile hotel room. Even when I was out, I kept to myself. Having decided I would be staying in Barcelona indefinitely, I didn't need or want to draw unnecessary attention toward myself. It was a huge risk just being with Livvie.

It didn't take long for Livvie's friends to realize something had changed. She'd all but abandoned them those first three weeks. She worked three nights a week and went to school Monday through Thursday. She spent most of her free time with me.

"So," Livvie began as we sat down to eat the meal room service had brought up. "Remember when we said we'd take things one day at a time and figure out what we were going to tell people when the time came?" She bit into a piece of asparagus. I swallowed the chunk of steak in my mouth without chewing.

"Yes."

"Well, I think we should start talking about it. Claudia and Rubi are starting to complain about the amount of time I'm *not* spending with them." She smiled at me.

I stabbed a piece of broccoli like it owed me money.

"Why is it their business? You're an adult. You don't need their permission to see me."

"Caleb," she admonished. "They're my friends. They've been there for me. If you're going to fit into my life, you're going to have to find a way to get to know my friends. I can't keep coming over here every night. It's exhausting. I have a life!"

"And aren't you lucky? Good for you." I shoveled food into my mouth and avoided her eyes. I didn't know why I was so angry. She'd made a perfectly valid argument and I'd shit on it. Her smile quickly disappeared.

"You know what? How about I just quit my job?" she spat.

I looked up from my plate. *Here we go...*

"Livvie—"

"No!" She was on a roll. Her eyes screamed of crazy. "It's perfect! I'll leave school and cut my friends out of my life. Then you can have me all to yourself! You can keep me in your dark little room and fuck me stupid. You can *own* me. It's what you want, isn't it?"

My rage was a living, breathing monster in my gut and it fed on every word she'd said. I had no doubt she'd been waiting to say those words to me since the night we'd talked on her balcony. Did her words hurt? Yes. But they also excited me. My dick was hard and a familiar thrumming thudded in my ears. I wanted a fight. I *needed* a fight. I was sick and tired of playing nice. I AM NOT NICE!

I chewed my food slowly and with a smile on my face. I watched Livvie closely. She was trying hard not to crack under the pressure of my silence. Livvie could never handle it—*still* can't. I could hear her breathing. Her eyes were narrowed onto my face. If I'd been some little boy her age, I might have worried for my safety. But I'd seen scary, and Livvie just didn't fit the bill. She was too sweet, too sexy.

"Aren't you going to fucking respond?" She was taunting me and enjoying it. Her chest rose and fell with gaining speed. I could make out the points of her nipples through her shirt.

I swallowed my food and sipped from my wine glass. I'd missed the familiarity of pushing Livvie's buttons. I didn't want to hurt her. I'd vowed not to hurt her again. It didn't mean I had to become a pussy.

"You want a response, Kitten?" Fear flickered just behind her angry stare. She shivered before she could stop it. I took my napkin from my lap and set it on the table. Livvie watched me intently. "Here's my response."

I slid my arm across the table. Our plates, glasses, and silverware crashed onto the floor. I stood up just in time to catch Livvie's arm as she leapt out of her chair and ran toward the door.

"Caleb, no!" she screamed. I put my hand across her mouth and hoisted her with one arm. Her legs kicked out at me viciously. Her teeth bit into my hand. Her nails dug into the flesh of my arm. The pain only spurred me on.

I pressed her body into the wall until she could barely move. She squirmed against me. You might hate me for it, but I loved every second. Then again, I knew I wasn't going to hurt her—not really. Once I had her immobilized, I whispered into her ear.

"Don't you think if that's what I wanted, I wouldn't just do it?" She whimpered. "It would be easier for me. You'd be mine in every way possible." I rubbed my cock between the cheeks of her ass. I almost came in my pants when she groaned. She struggled, but she was barely trying.

"I could keep you chained to the bed. I'd fuck you every night and never let you come. Only good girls get to come, Kitten. Would you be a good girl for me?" I took my hand away from Livvie's mouth and smoothed her hair back so I could see the side of her face.

"Fuck you. Let me go," she panted. Her tone meant business, but her body language told another story. She moved against my cock.

We were in dangerous territory. I knew the situation could blow up in my face, but the thrill was too strong. I couldn't resist. I pressed her deeper into the wall, until she gasped for breath. I planted soft kisses against her neck.

"I'll let you go if you're not wet," I whispered into her ear.

She didn't move. She didn't speak.

"What, no response? Should I check?" My heart was racing. I was afraid of going too far. I was afraid I'd *already* gone too far and didn't know how to come back. "Tell me to stop and I will. Tell me you don't want me to pull your tights down and fuck you up against this wall. Remind me of what a terrible person I am. Tell me I'm a sick bastard and you want me out of your life forever."

Livvie screwed her eyes shut. Her lip trembled, but she didn't cry.

I softened toward her. I didn't want to hurt her. I loved her. I didn't know how to do it like normal people. I didn't know how to tell her how scared I was. I pressed my forehead to the back of her neck and I tried.

"Tell me I don't deserve you. Tell me all the things I already know."

"Caleb..." My name was a heart-wrenching sound coming from her lips. I prepared for the worst and began to pull away. Livvie's hands gripped my forearm and held me in place. "Fuck me."

There was no time to think. I reacted. I pulled her skirt up to her waist. I shoved her panties and tights down to her knees. She gasped. Her hands slapped against the wall for balance. It was only seconds before I had my own pants down to my ankles. I thrust into Livvie fast and hard.

She was wet. She was wet and warm and fucking heaven wrapped around me. I never wanted to leave the safety of her body. As long as I was inside her, she was *mine.* No one could take her from me. I couldn't ruin things between us.

I pounded away at her. I put my hands around her wrists and fucked her into the wall. I practically lifted her body with every thrust... and I groveled.

"I'm sorry, Livvie. I'm sorry. Forgive me. Forgive me." And I kept fucking.

Afterward, Livvie left in a hurry. I was tempted to stop her, but I didn't. I felt I'd done enough damage for one night. I left all the broken dishes on the floor and proceeded to take a scalding hot shower. I refused to sleep that night.

Early the next morning, Livvie called me.

"Hey you." I could hear the smile in her voice. I was a little suspicious but warily accepted she might not be mad about the night before.

I rubbed my eyes. I was exhausted.

"Hey."

"I just wanted to let you know I have work after class, but I'm free tomorrow. I can spend the night, and tomorrow I thought we could go see a movie. I want to watch *Let Me In.*"

I sat up and propped myself up against the head-board.

"Um... okay." I'd been expecting anger from her. Maybe even excuses as to why she couldn't see me for a while. I decided it was better to accept her offer than question her motives. "What's it about?"

"It's sort of a horror movie, but not really. I really liked the Swedish version called *Let the Right One In*, but I'm curious to see what the director did with it."

I smiled. I remembered all the movie posters in her apartment.

"Of course, Livvie. We can do that."

"No pet names today?" she teased.

"I thought you didn't like it."

There was silence on her end. Then very quietly, "I liked it last night."

My dick stirred.

"Good to know."

"Yeah, well… just don't get too many ideas. You can't solve everything with sex, Caleb."

A tingle of shame bloomed in my chest.

"I'll try to remember."

"Good. See you tonight, Sexy."

I laughed. "Is that a pet name? I hate it."

"I'll try to remember."

I hung up and went straight to sleep. I didn't even dream.

CHAPTER SIX

Livvie liked to see a lot of movies and read a lot of books. She often lamented not being able to read as often as she'd like because her life was so busy between work, school, and dividing her free time between me and her friends. I often changed the subject when she brought up the last bit. I knew she wanted me to meet them. However, the idea of surrounding myself with typical twenty-year-olds was less than appealing. I had nothing in common with most people—less with those who had never shot a person at point-blank range. At least Livvie and I had *that* in common!

"Thanksgiving is next week," Livvie said as she slid into the car. We'd just finished watching *Harry Potter and the Deathly Hallows: Part 1*. Livvie had insisted we have a marathon to catch me up before we went to see the film. Surprisingly, I genuinely enjoyed the movies. I wondered if I was more like Harry or Voldemort. "Caleb."

"Yes?" I looked toward Livvie and smiled. She sighed.

"You know where I'm going with this. Don't make it difficult for me."

"Come on, Kitten. Again? I have enough friends. I don't want any more."

"You don't have any friends, Caleb."

"You're my friend." I winked at her as I started the car. She was a sucker for my flirting.

"Gah!" She threw up her hands sarcastically. "You are so irritating! If you weren't so handsome I'd punch you in the face." I laughed. "Come on, Caleb. Don't be an ass. I've been really patient, but this is important to me. *You're* important to me... and so are they. Please don't make me choose."

Despite her playful tone, I could tell how serious the situation truly was. I'd put her through a lot. After all, an evening with her friends had to bode better for me than it had for Livvie when she'd spent time with mine.

"What are we going to tell them about me?"

She shifted in her seat and gave me a look of tempered excitement.

"Ohmygod, are you asking me because you're actually considering it?" I rolled my eyes.

"I suppose," I grumbled. I wasn't prepared when Livvie took off her seatbelt and jumped on me with a squeal of delight. I tapped my brakes and heard a horn blaring behind me. "Livvie! What the fuck? I'm driving!" She was completely unapologetic.

"I'm so happy! So happy, happy, happy." She danced into her seat and put her seatbelt back on. "Claudia is going to flip her shit when she sees you. Rubi is super polite, but Claudia is a bit of a chatterbox. So expect her to talk your ear off. Sometimes she gets kinda personal, but I'll warn her ahead of time how grumpy you are. Ohmygod, what are we going to eat? I hope the grocery store has turkeys. Big turkeys!"

My anxiety levels were rising. What the hell had I just agreed to?

"Livvie, it's not going to be that easy. We have to be careful if you don't want to send me pen pal letters in prison."

Her excitement dwindled slightly. She rested her hand on my arm.

"We'd run before I ever let that happen, Caleb." She was dead serious. My chest felt a little tighter. "Besides," she continued, "the FBI is far from here and they don't check on me unless I reach out first. Sloan calls sometimes, but now that she knows I have friends and don't sit around moping over you, I don't hear from her much. We're okay, Caleb. We're perfect."

I smiled despite myself.

"We're pretty far from perfect, Kitten. I'm the most fucked up person you know."

"Yeah, but I'm the second most fucked up person I know, and when you put two negatives together, you get a positive. That's math, Caleb. Math is the language of the universe. You can't argue with the universe." Her grin was patently ridiculous.

I love you so goddamn much.

"Yes, well, I've been screwed over by the universe before."

"I know! It totally owes us." She stuck out her tongue. I laughed.

"Seriously, what are we going to say?" I held her hand as I focused on the road.

"Well, it's just like writing. You start with what you know, and what I know is the best lies are rooted in the truth. Your name is James. You were born in Portland, Oregon. You're twenty-seven, well-traveled, and we've been seeing each other for a month and a half."

I laughed.

"Been thinking about it, have you? My passport doesn't say James. Also, in the event your FBI friends come poking around, I'm not sure having James Cole in your life is going to go unnoticed. Then there's what do I do for a living? Why do I have an accent if I grew up in America? What's my family like? Do I have any hobbies?" I slowly watched the enthusiasm fade from Livvie's face. I felt like shit. "I'm sorry, Livvie. I know you deserve better, but I just don't know how you think we can pull this off."

She was quiet for the rest of the ride back to my hotel. We stripped and climbed into bed. I pulled her close. I could practically hear the gears turning in her head.

"We tell them we're both in witness protection," she said. "We aren't supposed to be together, but we couldn't stand to be apart. The FBI wants you to turn over evidence that belongs to another country. That's why Reed was poking around and I've been so secretive about where I'm spending my nights. They can never tell anyone about us. As far as they're concerned, we met at *The Paseo*. They love me, Caleb. They'll keep our secret."

I shook my head.

"Do you really think that will work? It seems far-fetched."

"No more so than the truth."

I considered her words carefully. It could work if her friends could truly be trusted, but I didn't know them from anyone. I'd have to check them out thoroughly, keep an eye on them. Livvie wouldn't like it. I'd have to keep it from her, but it was better than getting ambushed down the line. Rafiq was with me for twelve years before I found out he couldn't be trusted. I was never going to make that mistake again.

"We'll wait on telling them about witness protection. We'll avoid details beyond my name, where we met, and what I do. If all goes well, we can tell them the 'truth' later."

"What are you going to tell them about your job?"

"I'll tell them I'm independently wealthy. I have a trust fund. I've traveled since I was a boy and that's why my accent is strange. I'm twenty-seven, well-traveled, and we've been seeing each other for a month and a half." I kissed the top of Livvie's head.

"Thank you, Caleb."

"You're welcome, Kitten." I reached for her breast and traced her nipple with my thumb. I kissed her throat when she sighed, tilting her head to the side to allow me access. My hand slid from her breast, down her ribs, and over her ass until I palmed her flesh and squeezed. "You owe me though," I whispered against her neck.

"Mmm. What do you want?" She mimicked my actions and palmed my ass. She was oddly obsessed with my body. I couldn't complain.

"I want several things." I sucked the flesh of her shoulder into my mouth. She arched her body against me, rubbing her tits against my chest. Her fingers dug into the flesh of my ass. "Let's start with you moving your hand and putting it somewhere a little more useful." She giggled softly.

"I like where it is." She spanked me. It was loud, but it didn't hurt. I laughed.

"In your fucking dreams, Kitten. But if it's spanking you enjoy, allow me to indulge you." I let my hand fall on her ass solidly. The force caused her to push closer to me.

"No!" she yelped and squirmed in my grasp. "No, Caleb. I swear to God!" She was laughing, but also panicked. I let her go and she did exactly as I'd hoped—she ran. Her naked body bounded over me onto the floor and she took off toward the living room with a squeal.

I gave chase.

"You're going to make security come up here," I taunted from one side of the sofa. Livvie was on the other side, countering every move I made in either direction. She was laughing maniacally, half excited, half frightened.

"Good. I'll tell them you're trying to spank me. Pervert!"

"You love it. You're the pervert!" I pushed the sofa toward her, upsetting her balance. I lunged, but she backed away and made a run toward the dining room table. I paid an ungodly amount for the room. I didn't give a shit if we destroyed it.

"Stop chasing me!"

"Stop running."

She circled the table, tossing down the chairs as she went. Her nipples were hard little pebbles I couldn't keep my eyes from as her full breasts jiggled and swayed with her movements.

"You promise not to spank me?"

I grinned.

"Not a fucking chance." I watched her carefully as she kept going around the table, stepping over the backs of the chairs she'd knocked over. If I made my move too soon, she could run toward the bedroom and subsequently lock herself in the bathroom. On the other side of the table, her back was to the wall. I let her enjoy the thrill of evading me for one last turn around the table. I leapt on top of the table, startling her. She backed up and hit the wall with her back. I jumped down and pinned her.

"Gotcha."

She was breathing hard. I loved watching her laugh when she was trying hard not to. Despite her obvious beauty, she often made the most hideously comedic faces.

"What are you gonna do?" She wrapped her arms around my shoulders. She was suddenly very flirty.

"Whatever I want." I kissed her lips until she opened for me. As I swept my tongue inside I felt satisfaction in the way she moaned and rubbed herself against me. The idea that I had ever thought of giving her away was almost enough to make me angry. However, if being so close to Livvie had taught me anything (and it had taught me a great deal), it was that being angry was next to impossible while she melted against me.

In the weeks prior, I had learned that Livvie liked to play a little rough. It suited me well when I didn't overthink it. She liked to be held down and done from behind. She liked to be told what to do. She liked to be spanked. Mostly, though, she liked to come. She didn't care how it happened—just that it did. It helped take the edge off for me.

I backed away, stroking my dick. I liked the way Livvie's eyes followed my hand. She really did like to watch me (so long as another woman wasn't in bed with me). Her lips were swollen from kissing. She licked them and waited. I obliged by shortening her wait.

"Put your hands on the table and spread your legs." She smiled wickedly.

"Yes, Caleb." She quickly assumed the position.

I ran my hand down her long ebony mane. I knew one day I would insist on wrapping it around my dick and coming in it. I brushed her hair aside and replayed my touch down her spine. I grinned when she dipped her chest lower, lifting her ass. I would get to it, but I took my time touching everything. Her tits looked heavier in her position—full. I pinched them and she whimpered. I pinched her clit and she moaned. Her moans and whimpers were like food for my dark soul.

"You ready for me to spank you?" It wasn't really a question. It was a warning. She took a deep breath and let it out slowly. Her breath hitched with anticipation.

"Yes, Caleb."

"Put your chest down on the table and hold the sides." I waited patiently for her to comply. Livvie's beautiful skin was free of imperfections. There were no scars marring her slender back. She'd been spared my fate and I was deeply grateful.

I braced her body against my hip with one hand. I delivered the first blow with my free hand. The sound rent the air. Livvie gasped, but otherwise remained silent. I watched her ass turn pink where my hand had been.

"Pink already, Pet. How many do you think it'll take for your ass to be bright red?"

"I don't know, Caleb." She spoke softly. Her legs trembled.

"Should we find out?" I traced the welt with my fingertip. Livvie whimpered again.

"If that's what you want, Caleb." I smiled to myself. I knew I was a sick fuck. Livvie made me a lucky fuck too. I spanked her twice, one slap after the other. Livvie braced with her arms, but didn't clench her ass. *Practice, practice, practice.*

"Is that good, Kitten?" My own breathing had picked up speed as my arousal shot through the roof. Livvie's sounds, coupled with her writhing, had me in an acute state of lust.

"Yes, Caleb. More please."

I hissed. I spanked her four times in rapid succession. Livvie's ass was hot beneath my fingers. She picked up her feet and writhed against the table.

"Getting pretty red now, Pet." I was panting. "Put those fucking feet on the ground. You know better."

"Yes, Caleb," Livvie whispered. She was close to tears. She wouldn't be able to take much more. Hell, I couldn't take much more.

I used my heated fingers to rub her pussy from behind. She moaned and opened her legs wider.

"You're awfully wet inside, Kitten. You must really like getting a spanking." I slid my index finger inside her and moved it back and forth slowly. She shook.

"I like this better. More please. Harder." She started moving her hips as much as she could with me holding her. She was fucking herself with my finger.

"You're not being a very good pet right now, Kitten. You don't get to decide when you get fucked." I slowed my finger and she groaned in frustration. I smiled. "Who decides, Kitten?"

"You do, Caleb." She went still and relaxed her all her muscles. She was a vessel for my pleasure, a willing participant in my depravity.

"That's right, Kitten. I do." I spanked her three more times before I heard a little sob. She'd had enough. I'd had enough. I stood behind her, lifted her hips, and slid her wet pussy down my cock until I hit the bottom of her.

"Oh, god! Please, Caleb." She took swift advantage of the table and used it as leverage to saw herself back and forth on my cock. It felt so good, I temporarily gave up control. It couldn't last long. It wasn't what either of us wanted. I wanted control. Livvie wanted to surrender it.

Gaining my wits, I laid down on top of her. I'm over six feet tall (I use feet for your benefit, but you should really learn metric, America) to Livvie's five feet six. I covered her entire body. To avoid depleting her oxygen supply, I braced on one elbow and gripped the other end of the table with my free hand.

"You want it hard, Pet? I'll give it to you." I moved my hips in long strokes, almost pulling out when I moved back, making Livvie grunt when I gave her all of me at once on the way forward.

We did it that way until my elbow hurt and we were dripping with sweat, then I flipped us over and made Livvie ride me until we both came.

She fell asleep on top of me afterward. My dick was still inside her, getting soft. Semen ran out whenever either of us moved. I didn't care. I was too damn happy.

CHAPTER SEVEN

The night before Thanksgiving, I had a dream Livvie said she'd decided she couldn't love me. I woke up in a panic and made Livvie have sex with me. She didn't seem to mind.

We had Thanksgiving dinner in Livvie's apartment. Claudia and Rubio brought bottles of sangria, since it was apparently the favorite drink of their little group. I started drinking scotch before breakfast.

Livvie thought it was "cute" how nervous I was. True, I was a little nervous, but mostly I wasn't looking forward to making conversation. I figured the smell of me might keep people away.

Claudia was a force of nature—a spritely-looking creature with short dark hair, green eyes, and a mischievously sinister grin. She was even smaller than Livvie, but you wouldn't notice it given the way she had a tendency to get into one's personal space. That *one* being me.

"Oh my god, you're gorgeous." She held my head in both hands and turned my face from side to side, then up toward the ceiling. I felt like I was being looked over for lice, or worse—being appraised. I pulled my face away and scowled at her. "Oh! Touchy. Sophia said you were." She shrugged and hopped toward the kitchen.

Rubio was much more respectful. He was handsome in an awkward sort of way. He was tall, but lanky. His hair had a fastidiously cultivated look of dishevelment, as was the style with the youth in Europe. He shared the same color eyes as his girlfriend.

I had no doubt as to who ran the relationship between Claudia and Rubio. At the very least, Rubio had the decency to look embarrassed.

"Sorry, she does that to everybody. When I met her, she told me I was adorable and was her boyfriend."

"And you became her boyfriend?" I gave him a look. He smiled.

"She was wearing a tight shirt and I could see her boobs."

I couldn't help but smile.

"You did the right thing."

"I know." He shrugged.

Thanksgiving is an American holiday. Livvie and I had to scour the grocery stores to find a turkey that was apparently suitable enough to feed an army, despite our only needing to feed four people. However, as I watched Livvie pull the turkey out of the oven and set it on top of the stove, I knew it had been time well spent. Livvie's pride in her poultry was unmistakable.

"Look! It's my first turkey." Livvie showcased the bird between her outstretched hands with a curtsy.

"Is it supposed to be swimming?" I asked. It smelled delicious and I couldn't wait to eat it, but I love to give Livvie shit. It's my second favorite pastime.

"I hate dry turkey. I may have over-basted it. Who am I kidding, though? No such thing. You'll eat my fucking turkey and lick your fingers when you're done." She pulled a strip of meat off the top of the turkey and put it to my lips. "Open up, lover."

I put my arm around her and pulled. She smelled of perfume and food. I opened my mouth and let her feed me. It was the best turkey I'd ever had—moist inside with crispy skin. I licked Livvie's fingers as she withdrew.

"Hmm, not bad. You almost didn't get your finger back."

Livvie beamed at me.

"Well, I'm a lucky girl then. There's so much I like to do with my fingers." She pulled my mouth toward hers and kissed me. Between us, my cock gave a twitch. Livvie pulled away slowly with one last peck against my lips. "Claudia and Rubi are here."

I rubbed the front of my pants against her belly. Our height difference always confused my cock. It couldn't decide between seeking the warmth between her breasts and the wet heat waiting just below.

"They can watch. The boy might learn something."

Livvie laughed and pulled away.

"Not everyone is as obsessed with sex as you are. I don't think they'd appreciate it very much."

I shrugged.

"We could ask."

Just then, the sprite walked into the crowded kitchen.

"Tell me the food is ready! I am starving. I didn't eat all day because you said to come hungry." She grabbed a roll from a nearby pan and started munching. "Mmm, this one is still hot." She crammed the rest into her mouth.

"Claudia! That's not for snacking, you bitch." Livvie spanked the other girl on the ass and both of them giggled.

Girls are so strange. If another man called me a bitch and spanked me, it would not end in giggles. Although, women are far more inherently bisexual than men in my opinion. The thought gave me pause as I pictured Livvie doing very dirty things to the sprite. I turned toward the living room and made my escape before my dick got any harder. The kitchen was crowded enough.

Rubio was in the living room unraveling cords and setting up the PlayStation when I walked in. I was surprised he could do any amount of labor wearing the pants he had on. I don't understand skinny jeans for men. Who wants to walk around with their balls in a vise? For a second I wondered what Rafiq would think of the fad. A strange sort of melancholy drifted through me and I set my scotch on the coffee table. The last thing I needed was drunken reflection.

"Do you need help with that?" I asked. I needed a distraction.

"No, I got it already. Do you play or sing?" He beamed at me and I suddenly felt very old and out of touch with the world I was invading.

"Neither," I said. I stood there feeling awkward without a drink in my hand and with nothing to do. Rubio smiled and put a plastic guitar in my hand.

"You can start with the guitar. It's easier if you're just starting." He didn't wait for my reply before he turned on the TV and loud rock music filled the living room. I found it annoying but didn't say anything about it.

"What do I do?" I asked.

"You have to choose a character first. Then we pick a song and you push the colored buttons on the guitar as they go by on the screen. I'm going to play the drums." Rubio seemed excited and I didn't understand it. I'd never considered myself socially retarded until that moment.

I chose a bearded rocker as my character and got a feel for the toy guitar in my hands. At the very least, I felt less awkward having something to do. Rubio selected his character and proceeded to the song list.

"What's the name of our band?"

"Sophia picked it. We're The Sex Rifles." He laughed. "She thought it was more gangster than The Sex Pistols." I didn't know who The Sex Pistols were, but I could appreciate Livvie's sense of humor.

"Ooh, yes! I want to play." Claudia squealed as she joined us in the living room. I looked around for Livvie and didn't see her. *Please don't leave me alone with both of them.*

"Where's L-Sophia?" I just stopped myself from saying Livvie and was glad the pair of them were too busy fitting Claudia with a bass guitar.

"Sophia! Come play!" Claudia yelled at an obnoxious level. I must have made a face because she responded to me. "Get used to it, gorgeous man. If you're going to be part of our group, you're going to have to handle our rude-ass behavior. There's no room for politeness in a family." She winked at me. I smiled.

"You startled me is all; I don't think you're rude." Really, she was very rude. If she weren't Livvie's friend, I'd have shown her some manners. Alas, I had promised Livvie I was done torturing people who didn't like it. And as for family, she was really talking to the wrong person.

Livvie walked in and the happiness I saw on her face melted me. I wasn't sure I'd ever seen her so happy. It made me jealous of her friends. I'd given up my whole fucking life to be with her and she never looked that happy with me. She walked up to me and fiddled with the strap of the guitar.

"Well, look at you. You making nice, Sexy?" She rose up on her toes and puckered her lips. I bent down and accepted her kiss without thinking.

"I have a name, you know."

She grinned.

"I remember, Sexy." She turned and reached for the controller and the microphone. "Dinner is ready, so we can only do one or two songs and then we should eat."

"The food is so good, Rubi. I'm glad you met me instead of Sophia first. I'll never make you anything that good," Claudia said.

"What you give me is better than food," Rubio replied evenly. He kissed his girlfriend on the cheek and she blushed. I gained a little respect for them both. Their love was obvious and I hoped that one day Livvie and I could have what they did... without the skinny jeans... or the reminder we met under horrendous circumstances.

I felt a tap against my ass. Livvie was giving me some serious "come fuck me" eyes.

"You ready to play, Sexy? Make sure you set it to easy so you don't hurt yourself."

Some of my anxiety fell away.

"And you better remember who you're talking to, or else I'll have to remind you."

"Oh, I look forward to it." She squeezed my ass. I shook my head and laughed. "Okay, I'm gonna do 'Eye of the Tiger'."

"You always do that one," Claudia whined.

"Shut up! When it's your turn to sing, you can pick the song. Don't embarrass me in front of Sexy. I want him to marvel at how talented I am," Livvie said.

"You should let him read your smut. I bet he'd love that." Claudia made claws out of her fingers and scratched at the air in a motion no one in their right mind would think is sexy but was supposed to be.

"Is that what you're always writing on your laptop?" I smiled wide, knowing I was going to get my hands on Livvie's laptop at my earliest opportunity. Livvie looked ashen for a second.

"It's nothing. Forget it. Let's play already."

"Oh come on, Sophia. It's so good." She turned to me. "It's about this girl who—"

"Claudia!" Livvie said seriously and glared.

"Fine. Okay, let's play," Claudia said sarcastically.

My interest was piqued before, but I became like a dog with a bone after Livvie's reaction. I would be asking questions later, that much was certain. For the moment, I decided to focus on the plastic guitar in my hands and pushing the right buttons. It was a good thing my mind is so quick, because even on medium I was having a tough time keeping up with the rush of colors going across the screen.

The intro seemed to take forever, but once Livvie began singing I found myself swept up in the game. Livvie's voice was beautiful, raspy and powerful. She seemed filled with so many talents I didn't know about. I wanted to know all there was to know about her. I fleetingly wondered what talents I possessed that could possibly compare with hers. She turned toward me during an instrumental section.

"You're doing good! I suck at guitar."

I winked at her.

"Trying to concentrate, Pet. If you don't mind."

"Ha! Play on, rock star, don't let me stop you." She went back to belting the chorus and I wondered how her lungs were capable of holding so much air.

Finally, the song ended and I skated through the round with a seventy-five percent success rate. The rest of the band scored in the nineties and Livvie the highest with ninety-nine percent. A fact she wouldn't stop gloating about. I'd never seen Livvie so smug, and I felt my chest expand with something akin to pride at seeing some of my own mannerisms in her. We'd come so far, and I was oddly desperate to see where we could go.

Claudia sang next. Her softer, more lyrical voice did well with "Nine in the Afternoon." I had a hard time keeping up with the guitar but seemed to be out-performing Livvie, who was attempting to play bass with her entire body. Her tongue was out as she concentrated on the screen, paying no attention to the way I stared at her every chance I had.

After Claudia finished her song and everyone laughed at my sixty-two percent accuracy (Livvie only had sixty-five, and why they chose to only make fun of me, I'll never know—bastards), the decision was made to sit down to dinner. Livvie's table wasn't large enough for all the food and guests, so we served ourselves in the kitchen and brought our plates to the table. It was all so strange to me. I felt a bit like an outsider, even if I'd literally been closer to Livvie than either of her friends.

Once everyone was seated, I picked up my fork, eager to get into the turkey and stuffing when Livvie stayed my hand. I looked at her and purposely growled. She only smiled and patted my hand.

"Not yet, Sexy. It's Thanksgiving. We have to go around and say what we're thankful for."

"I'd be thankful if we could eat," I muttered. I put my fork down and looked around the table. They were all smiling at me. It was creepy. Believe me—I know creepy.

"Sophia, it's your house. You should go first." Rubio suggested.

"Okay," Livvie said and took a deep breath. "Well, first, I want to say I'm thankful for the food. I can't wait to eat it. But, more importantly… I'm thankful that I'm here at all." She swallowed, and the sight of her eyes becoming wet with unshed tears made me want to tell everyone to leave so I could kiss her into forgetting everything she was feeling. Instead, I had to sit and pretend I wasn't the villain in Livvie's life. "It's been a difficult year for me. Last year I spent Thanksgiving alone. I didn't know where I was going with my life or what I wanted out of it anymore. I was… heartbroken and miserable." A tear rolled down her cheek.

"Sophia…." Claudia reached for Livvie across her boyfriend's chest. Livvie smiled.

"No, it's okay. I don't mean to cry. It's just… this year, I have two of the greatest friends a girl could ask for, an apartment of my own—in Spain! And I…" She looked toward me, and damn it I could feel myself getting caught up in her emotions. "I have you. I have a place to belong. I have a family that loves me. I'm deeply grateful for that. I don't know where I'd be without it." She wiped at her cheek and shook herself. "Eww, sorry to get all emo. I just love you fuckers, that's all. Someone else go now."

I sat perfectly still in my seat, trying to process exactly what I was feeling. Livvie had included me on her list. She was thankful for me. She'd found a place to belong with me. I felt exactly the same way, but I could never be so casual with expressing my emotions. Perhaps if we were alone, perhaps if we were in the dark, or imaginably naked, then I could tell her. But everyone was looking at me. Livvie was smiling sweetly, encouragingly. Claudia's stare was much more invasive and practically tried to intimidate me into speaking. Rubio simply waited. He was a patient sort. I cleared my throat and smiled.

"Well, it's difficult to top that, but I'll try to offer something." I looked toward Livvie. "I know we haven't known each other long. We've only been seeing each other a month and a half." She smiled at me with narrowed eyes. "However, I can honestly say… these have been the best six weeks I've ever had. I'm thankful for the time we've been given so far, and I hope that by next year—" I looked toward everyone else, "I'll love all you fuckers as well."

Claudia and Rubio laughed. I returned my gaze to Livvie. She was staring at me with an expression I hadn't quite seen before. I liked it.

"I'm thankful for good food, great friends, and love. May God bless this food and our friendships," Rubio said quickly and succinctly. I looked away from Livvie reluctantly and smiled. Claudia pulled Rubio toward her mouth roughly and kissed him much more passionately than was perhaps appropriate at the dinner table. Young love. That's what I wanted.

Claudia whispered to him in Spanish, "I'm thankful for you, my love." To the rest of the table, she said, "I'm thankful for my family, my friends, and all this food. Now please, let's eat it!" Everyone laughed and agreed it was time to eat. I picked up my fork and dove into the turkey and stuffing. It was my first Thanksgiving and I immediately decided we would celebrate it every year.

Over dinner, I listened to Livvie discuss classes with her friends and the movies they were watching. They had been watching Stanley Kubrick's work and discussing it in class. Claudia and Rubio were fans, but Livvie felt a lot of his work lacked in its ability to communicate a clear message to its audience.

"All this talk about *A Clockwork Orange*, like it's the greatest movie ever or something," Livvie said around the turkey in her mouth. "I'd say two-thirds of the people who saw that movie didn't fucking get it. It's the emperor who has no clothes. Enough people called it brilliant that the idiots who didn't get it pretended to understand it just so they wouldn't be called idiots—which makes them cowardly idiots. The movie could have been better. It could have delivered the message of the movie in a much clearer fashion and inspired some real dialogue about human nature, society, and psychology as a treatment.

Instead, all anyone can remember is the rape scene. It's stupid."

"I have to disagree," said Rubio. "I think it's very clearly a movie about how society doesn't care about its own ruination. Society does not care about the disease—it only wants to treat the symptoms. It does not care that Alex is violent or what happened to make him such a sociopath. It only wants him punished and 'rehabilitated'. But there is no such thing as behavior control. It has to be a choice, a person has to choose to be a better person, and the only reason they choose to be better is if there is a reason. Alex was forcibly rehabilitated with aversion therapy, but once he went back out into the world and encountered all the violence that was still out there he became violent again. It's the nature of human beings. Kubrick did an incredible job."

"I know what the movie was about, Rubi. I get the point. *My* point is Kubrick was so obsessed with portraying the dystopian future that he neglected to push the message to a mainstream audience. Film students and artistic types are not typically prone to violence. The message is nothing new for them. The average moviegoer has to be kicked in the face with the truth or they don't fucking get it. Why do you think Mel Gibson's *The Passion of the Christ* did so well? It was like a hammer of guilt hitting people in the face."

"Fuck Mel Gibson!" Claudia contributed. "I don't care if he's talented. He's a sanctimonious ass and the last person with any right to make a movie about Jesus." Rubio caressed Claudia's arm.

"No need to get worked up, Claudia. We're just talking." Rubio looked toward me. "What do you think, James? Are you a Kubrick fan?"

It was the first time anyone had called me James. It was such a simple name. It had no hidden meaning like *dog* or *loyal disciple*. It was just a name. A normal name for a normal person.

"Um, I've never seen the movie and I don't really know who Kubrick is. We saw the new *Harry Potter* last week. I liked that one." I smiled and sipped some sangria. Everyone burst into laughter, and Livvie leaned over to give me another easy kiss.

"I'm sorry, Sexy. Sometimes we get our nerd on without thinking about other people. Let's change the subject."

"I don't mind. I like hearing what you think. I follow the conversation. Personally, I'd like to think a person can change for the better. But I think Rubio is correct as well—a person has to have a reason to change. They have to believe their situation will be made better by changing. Otherwise, that person is at a disadvantage. Violence is necessary if you live in a violent world." My heart was thumping hard.

Rubio's expression turned sour. "I never said violence was necessary. I said there's too much of it and we need to find a way to treat it as a societal disease."

"That will never happen. Even flowers kill, Rubio. Human beings are far more flawed than flowers. We all do what we feel we must do. If that means killing... so be it. Survival—"

"Is the most important thing," Livvie finished. Her expression turned wistful. She set her fork down and stood. "I'm bored of this conversation. Let's play more Rock Band." She smiled, but it didn't reach her eyes. I knew that smile well.

I regretted ever opening my stupid mouth.

We played Rock Band for a few more hours. I got much better at the guitar and actually enjoyed myself. I'd studied a lot of things about America and Americans. I'd learned about their pop culture, but I'd never played a video game. It was very entertaining and I decided I'd be buying a PlayStation the very next day.

Afterward, Claudia and Rubio decided to pack up more than their share of the leftovers and head home. They hugged me goodbye—yes, both of them—and I thought it was a little strange. I went with it, though. I could be a hugger... maybe. No, it was weird.

"If we were in The States, you could buy one on the cheap tomorrow. Too bad Spain doesn't celebrate Black Friday," Livvie said as she turned the faucet on and began washing dishes.

"What the hell is that?" I asked and opened the dishwasher.

"It's a sacred tradition where thousands of hoarders camp outside stores and then bludgeon their neighbors for the best prices on PlayStations and iPads. I used to go with my mom." She shrugged.

"I think I'll just order one on the computer. Unless you would find it romantic for me to bludgeon your neighbors?" I smiled. Livvie laughed.

"Hmmm... maybe. Let's see who complains about the loud rock music." She shoved me with her shoulder. "You did good today. My friends are a little in love with you, I think."

I felt a strange pang in my chest.

"I did my best. They seem nice. Claudia is a little too friendly, and I don't understand how Rubio does anything in those skinny pants, but they obviously love you. You're very lucky, Kitten." I paused. "There seems to be no shortage of people who love you."

Livvie was scouring a pot and didn't meet my eyes. "Caleb," she sighed.

"I like James. Maybe you should call me that. Less chance you'll slip around your friends. I could call you Sophia. We could, I don't know… pretend. We could pretend to be normal… together. I'm not wearing those skinny jeans, though." I tried to keep the conversation light. We'd had such a great day and I didn't want to ruin it.

Livvie handed me the pot for rinsing.

"I've been thinking about that. I think… it could be a good idea. It might sound weird, but when they changed my name I felt free to become someone else. Livvie was a sad girl. She cared too much about things that didn't matter and let people take advantage of her. Sophia is self-aware and she doesn't take shit from anyone."

I didn't care for her words.

"You never took shit from anyone. You're the strongest person I know. Stronger than me." I swallowed. "But I know what you mean. Rafiq started calling me Caleb after he…" I couldn't say the word rescued. Rafiq had never rescued me. "I used to be called something far less flattering."

Livvie handed me another dish and moved closer to me. Our arms brushed whenever we moved.

"What was it?"

I mentioned the name in Arabic.

"That doesn't sound bad. What's wrong with it?"

I had to laugh to keep from feeling everything else.

"It means dog. My name was dog." I took the dish Livvie had been washing from her hands and rinsed it before putting it in the dishwasher. I didn't want to acknowledge her shock.

"Why would anyone…? The world is fucking disgusting." She stopped washing dishes and put her arms around my waist from behind. "I think you're a miracle, James. I think you deserve to be happy. We both do."

I kept washing dishes.

"I don't know if you're right, Sophia. I know you deserve to be happy. I know you deserve someone… better, but I'm selfish. I want you. I want you bad enough to try and be someone better.

"That said, it wouldn't surprise me if you decided it was too little, too late. I won't be here a second longer than you want me to be. I promise." I didn't mention the part where I'd lose my fucking mind. I wasn't sure what I would do if Livvie didn't want to be with me. I didn't necessarily have anything to go back to except killing and smuggling. Was I a better person? Maybe not. I was only better when I was living for her. I felt like a time-bomb.

"Then I'm selfish too, because I want you just as much. I know it's been odd between us. How could it not be? We don't know each other in this world, but I've seen you at your worst, and what I know is that you'd do anything to protect me. That's enough for now. The rest will come." She kissed my back and came back to the sink to continue washing.

"There's not much to me, you know? Not much that's good anyway. What else do you expect to learn?" I knew my expression wasn't doing much to hide my frustration.

"I know we both like Harry Potter. I know you have to get drunk to meet my friends because you're nervous. You pay attention when you're not speaking and whenever you do, you add something to the conversation. You like to read as much as I do. I know I'll never catch you in a pair of skinny jeans." She laughed and bumped me with her hip. "I know you're a quick learner. You killed it on guitar in just a few hours. You help with dishes. I'm learning a lot of things about you, James. I like it."

"This is the part where I'd grab you and fuck you in front of the sink, but I have to be honest—I am stuffed! I can't wait to put on a pair of lounging pants and take a nap."

We laughed.

"That's the turkey. It makes everyone sleepy. Tomorrow we get to eat leftovers all day. So good." She looked at me sidelong and made her lips curve into a mischievous smile. "I'll be sure to ask you to fuck me before I feed you."

"Ask me?" I asked through a laugh. She'd never have to ask me.

"Beg you?" she purred.

My cock stirred.

"Well, I guess you *do* know me."

CHAPTER EIGHT

"Do you have plans for Christmas?" I asked Livvie. She handed me a cup of coffee and took a sip of her own. The temperature had been dropping steadily, but the streets were still crowded with would-be shoppers. Livvie and I seemed a bit at odds with our surroundings due to our lack of shopping bags. She smiled at me brightly.

"Yes. I plan to spend the better part of the day super glued to your body." She ran one of her mitten-clad hands down the front of my coat. I laughed.

"Well then, I'm looking forward to it already. I'll be sure to giftwrap." I tugged her close and kissed her more passionately than was appropriate in public. Her lips were cold but the inside of her mouth was warm and tasted faintly of coffee and sugar. "But I meant with other people. Are there people you have to see?"

A strange expression marred her features.

"No. It's just us. Claudia and Rubio are each spending time with their families. They're only going to see each other for part of the day because Rubio's family lives in Madrid. Claudia invited us to go over to her mom's house, but I didn't figure you'd want to go. Honestly, I don't feel like going either. We might all get together on Christmas Eve, though. Why do you ask?"

I took her hand and led her into the flow of bodies, making our way toward the next block of shopping. It had been her idea to go shopping, but Livvie had yet to purchase a single thing.

"I've never celebrated Christmas. I haven't celebrated a lot of holidays, actually. I thought since I liked your Thanksgiving, I might... branch out."

"Oh yeah?" Livvie said excitedly. "That's great, Sexy! Now I feel bad for not getting you a gift yet. We'll have to do it up right if it's your first Christmas. I figured you didn't celebrate it, so I didn't want to push the subject. If you weren't into it, no reason for me to celebrate."

I noticed the undercurrent of sadness in Livvie's voice and suspected it had something to do with her lack of family. I was oddly tempted to ask about them. I didn't much care for her mother, but I knew she had siblings and I didn't know if she spoke to them or not. Then again, her having a relationship with her family didn't necessarily bode well for me.

"You've already given me more than I've ever had. You wouldn't want to spoil me, would you?" I flashed my most suggestive grin. Livvie looked at me sidelong.

"I wouldn't *dream* of spoiling you. You're a big enough pain as it is."

"I'm sorry, I thought I was gentle." I braced for the punch I knew I was coming. She can be such a violent little thing.

"Don't be gross!" she admonished. It was difficult to take her seriously while she was laughing. "I wonder if there's still time to get a tree. Usually people put them up after Thanksgiving, but there has to be a lot somewhere that sells them. I'll ask Claudia. She usually knows where to go for stuff. I mean, I've learned a bunch since I've been here, but like, I'm not *from* here so I need help sometimes. Ha! This one time I got lost…" Livvie seemed completely engrossed in the art of one-sided conversation. I admit it, I tuned out a little. I thought I had learned the various sides to Livvie while in Mexico, but I was beginning to feel as though I'd only scratched the surface. I rather liked the idea of new discoveries—even when the discovery was that Livvie could be as much of a rambler as Claudia.

"I was thinking of something else entirely," I broke in. Livvie halted, much to the chagrin of the pedestrians behind us trying to get upstream with the other salmon.

"What were you thinking?" She looked somewhat perturbed and I wasn't sure why.

"What's that face for?"

She shook her head and pasted on a saccharine smile.

"Nothing. *Nothing*. It's just... what were you going to say?" She smiled a bit more genuinely.

"You were thinking something. Just tell me what it was." I took a sip from my coffee. I'd never been much of a coffee drinker, but it was slowly growing on me. Livvie usually had some with her breakfast. She blew out a breath.

"I don't know, I thought you might say something about... visiting friends of yours. Or something."

"Wow," I said. "You think I have friends? Friends I would want to spend holidays with, no less." I had to laugh out loud at the ridiculousness of it.

"Well, not friends, but... you know people." She lifted an ebony brow and tilted her head to the side with suspicion.

"I've left all that behind, Livvie. You know that," I said evenly.

"I thought you were going to call me Sophia from now on." She looked down at her shoe and kicked at an imaginary rock.

"That question wasn't exactly meant for James, was it?" I kept my tone pleasant.

"You're right. I'm sorry, James." She stepped closer and playfully kicked at the tip of my shoe with her sneakered foot. "You forgive me? Do I still get my surprise?"

I chuckled because I had no other recourse. I had come to understand our relationship would be riddled with moments where the past sucked all the joy out of the present. My only hope was that with enough time, Livvie and I would build memories capable of trumping our beginning.

"Yes, on both counts. I'm much too excited about your gift to let you ruin it for us."

Livvie looked up at me with a glare that quickly became a smile.

"It's for both of us, eh? It's not lingerie, is it? Because that's more for you than it is me. I'm not saying I won't wear it, but I'm going to insist I get other presents too."

"You're ridiculous." I started walking and Livvie quickly fell into step next to me.

"You're sexy," she whispered as she dragged my arm across her shoulders. It made for awkward walking, but I didn't mind.

"Yes, I know. It's a curse. Anyway, I was hoping you could take the week of Christmas off from work. I want to take you to Paris." I pulled her close and placed a kiss on the top of her head. The pink fuzz from her hat stuck to my lips. I lifted my arm from her shoulders and picked it off.

From the corner of my eye, I observed an older man watching me and Livvie. I wouldn't have noticed him, except he was alone and without shopping bags—or anything in his hands at all. He caught me watching and tilted his head in greeting before turning to look at a window display. I warily pulled my attention back toward Livvie. The old man wasn't anyone I knew and he hardly looked dangerous. I had left the world of intrigue behind. Old men were only old men.

"*Paris?* You are so damn sweet when you want to be. I've already been to Paris though—last year." She bounced as she walked happily. "I can probably get the time off work, though. It's late for requests, but Giovanni is pretty good about that kind of thing. I'm a student, so I don't think he expects too much out of me."

"Giovanni—is he handsome?" She seemed surrounded by men sometimes: Reed, Marco, Rubio, and now Giovanni.

"Only in that tall, dark, and foreign kind of way. Not my cuppa, really." She grinned.

"Asshole." I swatted her ass as we walked. People were beginning to stare at us while we walked. I thought of the old man and started to feel better about him watching us. It was more than possible that Livvie and I were simply drawing attention to ourselves. Some people even seemed to enjoy our antics. "Anyway, I know you've been to Paris before. I read about it in that email you sent to your friend."

"Don't remind me," Livvie said.

"I *am* reminding you. It didn't seem like you had very much fun while you were in Paris. You were lonely and some bastard stole your wallet. I thought we could go together and make new memories. I've never really played the tourist before. It could be fun. What do you think?" I took several swallows of coffee, pleased it had sufficiently cooled.

Livvie's eyes told me all I needed to know. They were bright and excited.

"I think… you're amazing, James. No one makes me as happy as you do." She hooked her arm in mine and rested her head on my arm. She let out a little sigh of contentment that warmed me better than the coffee.

"It's settled then. I'll make all the arrangements. We'll stay at the best hotel and eat at the best restaurants. We'll see all the best things and have the best sex." I was shockingly giddy. I'd never been the type before. I tried not to overthink it despite the niggling worry always running in the background of my thoughts that warned me how dangerous happiness could be.

"And I'll be with the best boyfriend ever!" Livvie did a little hop and spilled coffee onto her mitt and sleeve. "Ah, boo! My glove is all wet. Oh well, at least it didn't burn my hand."

We stopped at the next trash bin and tossed the coffee. Livvie stood still as I wiped her off as best I could with my gloved hands. Once finished, I pulled off my gloves and put them in the garbage along with hers.

"That's the first time you've called me your boyfriend," I mentioned softly. "We'll buy new gloves in that shop over there." I pointed. "It wouldn't hurt to find some outfits for Paris. I rather like the idea of you in lingerie." I bent down and kissed her lips. Livvie took it upon herself to deepen our affections by cupping the back of my head and pressing her lips once, twice, three times against my own until I opened my mouth to her tongue.

Livvie's kisses had gone from shy to ravenous during the course of our relationship. I was surprised to discover my growing taste for Livvie's forwardness. She'd had such a demure nature in the past and I'd loved to play The Wolf to her Little Red Riding Hood. I hoisted her up into my arms and she wrapped her legs around my waist. A mother hurried her children past and called us disgusting. I grabbed Livvie's ass and squeezed before I pulled away from the kiss and set her down. I tugged my coat down.

"I'd only kiss my boyfriend like that," she panted and giggled. I gave her one more kiss and managed to keep it chaste.

"I accept. These lips officially belong to me, and mine they will remain. If I find them anywhere near another man, he better be kin to you." I was entirely serious.

"You manage to say the most romantic things in the creepiest way possible. If I didn't know you, I'd be scared of you," she said with a smile and a wink.

"Oh, I'm still scary."

"Not to me," she whispered. I felt a little pinch in my chest.

"It's only acceptable from you." I tilted my chin toward the shop I had mentioned earlier. "Should we do some actual shopping on this shopping trip or are we only out to pervert young children?"

"Can't we do both?" she said with such seriousness I had to struggle to keep a straight face. Did other couples banter as much? I didn't think so.

We returned to Livvie's apartment with as many bags as we could manage. There had been some trepidation on Livvie's part over allowing me to pay for our purchases, but I was quick to point out it was my right as her boyfriend to shower her with gifts. I'd missed the opportunity to court her properly, I had said, and it was only fair to allow me to make up for it. I felt fifteen hundred Euros was a sufficient overture for one day.

She had purchased bags, shoes, cocktail dresses, new gloves, and enough lingerie to keep me ripping them off of her for a few weeks. There was a particular pair of lacy thong panties I couldn't wait to chew my way through. Oh, and a red negligee without breast cups that was of particular interest to me. I had looked for a red cape to go with it but came up empty. The urge to hunt down Little Red would have to wait.

"Are you hungry?" Livvie asked. I could barely hear her as I set the bags in the living room. Livvie had made her way toward the bedroom.

"Yes," I called out, "but I don't think you have anything in your cupboards worth—"

"Then get in here and eat my pussy!" Livvie interrupted.

"You little bitch," I muttered under my breath and laughed. She got me. "You're going to pay for that, Pet!" I yelled as I made my way toward the bedroom while divesting myself of my gloves, coat, and shirt. "I'm going to wash your filthy mouth out with cock." I heard the shower running in the adjoining bathroom. I kicked off my shoes, pulled on my belt, and slid the rest of my clothing down my legs and off.

"Ooooh, I'm soooo scared," Livvie taunted. She was already in the shower and soaping the parts I fully intended to put in my mouth. Ingredients for Mind-numbingly Sexy: 1 Livvie, Just add water.

I wasted no time once I stepped into the shower. I grabbed Livvie by her wet hair and tugged her back toward the shower wall. The water was hot and it stung my cold skin. I liked the burn.

"Who do you think you are, ordering me around? Didn't I teach you better?" I licked a hot, wet trail up the side of her neck while I slid my cock against her belly.

"It didn't stick," she panted hotly near my ear. "Teach me again."

Her words made my pulse race. There had been moments between us in Mexico when I had witnessed glimpses of Livvie's brazenness. However, that's exactly what they had been—glimpses. The Livvie I had been dating was worlds beyond the Livvie I had held captive. After a lifetime of being subjugated or, conversely, crushing the disobedience out of others, it shocked me how much I enjoyed the back and forth.

Yet, for all that Livvie seemed determined to push my buttons, her actions told a different tale. I was beginning to see that her words were less about putting me in my place and more about forcing me into a course of action that would lead me to behave... ungentlemanly.

"It's that mouth of yours." I kissed her softly and I could almost sense her annoyance after expecting something rougher. "It gets you into trouble every time." Another soft kiss, and another.

Livvie made frustrated little sounds. She tried to lean in and deepen the kiss but I selected that moment to remind her of my fist firmly embedded in her hair. She winced.

"Did that hurt?" I whispered against her lips and left another weak kiss. She made another frustrated sound and I felt the warmth of her hands on my hips urging me toward her. I lifted my free hand and traced her open lips with my fingertip. "I asked you a question, Pet. I expect you to answer it."

Livvie's fingers pressed deeper into my hips. Her eyes were gently closed. For whatever reason, she could never seem to handle the directness of my gaze. I allowed it only because I enjoyed the way she abandoned her self-control whenever she couldn't see. I thought of all the times I had blindfolded her to achieve the same results. Her tongue licked suggestively at my finger as it circled her lips. She had *never* been so blatant in Mexico, not without first being reminded of her need to survive. Things were different. She wanted me. She wanted to give herself to me. I felt unworthy to accept such a gift, but it didn't stop me from clutching it fiercely to my chest.

Long seconds passed without an answer.

"Do what you're going to do." Her voice was thick with lust.

I pulled her down by her hair slowly but with the force of my grip behind it. She went down easily, with only a small startled yelp to suggest her surprise.

"I said I was going to wash your mouth out with cock." I wrapped my hand around my hardened flesh and traced her lips with the tip. "Open up."

I licked my own lips as the lust thrumming though my body grew in intensity. I watched Livvie's lips purse defiantly. She placed soft kisses on the head of my cock and slowly worked down the shaft. It was nice to look at, but it offered no satisfaction. If she wanted a lesson, I was obliged to give her one. I tapped her face with my erection and she smiled wickedly. I gripped her hair rough and she gasped, allowing me to put myself inside.

Warmth. I was surrounded by it. It was a warmth that vibrated with every surprised murmur Livvie tried to make. I thrust into it in degrees. I watched as Livvie's lips stretched over my flesh and inches of me disappeared into the heat of her willing mouth. I delved deeper, until teeth scraped the sides of my cock and Livvie's throat contracted around me. *Yes! Right there.*

I know there are a lot of women who don't like sucking dick, but god, do I love the ones who do. For a moment I felt adrift in the sensation of Livvie's warm, wet, and tight mouth wrapped around my cock. The sensation was almost painful to pull away from. Every instinct in my body was *insisting* that I push harder, deeper, keep fucking—but I didn't. I pulled out quickly. Livvie was gasping. Loudly. A long trail of spit connected her flushed lips to the tip of my cock.

"More?" I asked. Livvie nodded and I pushed forward again. She sucked and my thighs started to quake.

There was only so much I could do to keep myself from getting too rough. I pulled my hands away from Livvie and my cock and placed them on the wall in front of me. I felt more than heard Livvie's grateful sigh. I was rewarded further when her hands roamed from my hips to my ass and she pulled me deeper into her mouth.

"Fuck!" I let myself stay. I wanted to stay. It felt so fucking good. Livvie's gag reflex kicked in and I pulled away quickly. More gasping. More spit.

Livvie opened her eyes as she caught her breath. There were tears in her eyes, but I knew she wasn't crying. She was wanton. Her head came forward and rubbed against my thigh in supplication. It's difficult to process all the things I feel when Livvie expresses herself this way. If I were a wolf, I would howl. If I were a lion, I would roar. If we lived in the jungle, I would bring her a wolf and a lion to feast on.

I reached down and stroked her wet head. She tilted her face into my hand, eyes pleading, her mouth leaving kisses in my palm. I had a thought: *Does she love* me, *or does she love all the things I do to her?*

"Tell me what you want," I said. It wasn't a question. Livvie's eyes had not left mine and it was easy to see the sudden vulnerability in them.

"To make you happy," she said. She seemed unsure, though I couldn't guess why.

"I'm happy," I said. I knew I could push her further, but I wasn't up for the repercussions. I pulled her up onto her shaky legs and finally gave her the proper kiss she'd been wanting. As I broke the kiss I said, "Turn around and spread your legs."

She did as I asked while I rearranged my larger frame in the small space. Livvie's shower was really only meant for one person. I managed to sit on the shower floor with her thighs spread over my face. I kissed her clit once before I slid my tongue inside her and made her come.

As she came apart above me, I guided her down my body until she finally sat on my cock. The void in me shuddered. It was enough, I told myself. Everything Livvie and I had was enough. I paid no attention to the void when it sang: *For now.*

Livvie and I kissed. We fucked.

The void was silent.

CHAPTER NINE

Paris is a lovely city, even in the winter. It's a delightful mix of the old and new. It's one of the only places you can see a five-hundred-year-old building with a Starbucks inside. However, as the world's most popular city to visit, the congestion of tourists does detract some from the experience. At least, it did for me. I don't like people as a general rule, and I like them even less when they're pressed against me in a crowded space.

It was our second day in Paris and Livvie had insisted that we visit the Louvre Museum. Thanks to some generous tipping, we managed to circumvent the line to see the *Mona Lisa* but not the throngs of people already inside.

"I wish we could see it better. All that glass makes it hard to see the details. Still pretty cool, though. What do you think?" Livvie looked up and craned her neck back to see me.

I scowled (it's something I do a lot apparently).

"I think this asshole behind me should take his blurry photo and stop bumping into me before I decide to do some performance art with his face."

Livvie's smile turned into a judgmental pout.

"It's crowded, Sexy. Guy can't help it. At least we're up front. Last time I was here, I was sort of in the middle and I couldn't see over the people. I kept getting pushed from every side. I finally just turned around and left." She leaned against the small barricade to get a closer look.

"Well, that idea has promise." I glared at the man behind me while Livvie wasn't looking. He held up his hand and dipped his head as he apologized. He was so nice about it I actually felt bad for being angry. This was the effect of being with Livvie. The old me would have said, *Yes, you're sorry. Now fuck off.*

There was a swat to my chest and I turned back toward Livvie, who had apparently caught me.

"Be. Nice. I don't want to be carted off to *Les Mis* jail in my fancy clothes. The *les*bians will eat me alive." She grinned.

"Two puns in one joke," I said with a blasé tone. "Bit of an overreach. Also, it's pronounced *lay*, not *les*."

"Whatever, it was funny." Livvie blushed and cuddled into my chest. I finally had to chuckle. It took me a long time to realize how adept Livvie is at managing my moods. She'd made me forget I was angry and she'd done it without my knowing.

I took her hand and navigated our way through the crowd so that we might visit other, less inhabited, exhibits. Like most people, I don't know art, but I know what I like. For my part, I appreciated some of the "less superior" pieces more than the *Mona Lisa*. I didn't find her smile that mysterious, to be honest. I enjoyed Guiseppe Arcimboldo's *Autumn* much more. The artist incorporated fruits and vegetables to create a portrait of a man. It made me think about life and death. All things ripen and die. I thought about being twenty-seven. Knowing one's age had consequences.

After the Louvre, we ate lunch at a small café within walking distance of the museum. The hotel provided a courtesy chauffeur, but Livvie insisted it was cheating to utilize such services. Walking was certainly more Parisian and therefore necessary to our tourist experience. I was no stranger to walking, but I shared no such thoughts on the subject.

By the time we reached the Eiffel Tower by way of the Arc de Triomphe, I was ready to throw Livvie into a taxi. But of course, we had to reach the top of the tower. Livvie—being the beautiful, young, and spry girl she is—

was still full of energy and smiles. It was just her luck (and my misfortune) that her joy seemed to be infectious and kept me from voicing my growing disdain for tourist traps.

"Awesome! The elevator is working this time," Livvie said.

I pulled her away from the ticket window before the line turned on her.

"Sorry, Kitten, but I'm not getting in that thing. What if it breaks down? Do you really want to be jammed into a tiny box with dozens of strangers? The idea doesn't appeal to me." I don't like cramped spaces of the non tight, wet, and warm variety.

"Aww, are you claustrophobic?" Livvie made a mockingly sad face.

"Watch yourself, Kitten. I'd hate to have to spank your ass in front of all these people." I tugged her close and delivered a firm slap to her behind. Someone giggled as they walked past. Livvie laughed.

"I can't believe you just did that."

"I plan on doing a lot more later," I whispered in her ear and bit it for good measure. She squealed and pulled away. "I just hope I have the energy after I climb all these damn stairs."

"Really? The stairs?" At last it was Livvie who was whining about doing things the hard way.

"Yes. The stairs. And it serves you right for having me walk all over Paris. I hope your thighs get nice and sore on the way up. It'll make things that much more interesting when I make you squat over me later." She scrunched up her nose and I laughed.

"You're mean," she said.

"Would you have me any other way?" I received little more than a suspicious glare. "Do you have anything in your coat pocket?"

She inspected her coat.

"No. All I brought was my passport, but you took it."

"Good. I'd hate for you to get pick-pocketed again." I kissed her forehead and directed our steps toward the stairs.

"What if you get pick-pocketed?"

"That's cute, Pet." I half hoped someone would try. I'd been growing increasingly desperate for confrontation. It had been months since I'd had some sort of altercation. I was surprised to discover how much I missed it. I pushed the thought aside for perhaps the hundredth time.

As others crammed themselves into the lift, Livvie and I started up the stairs. I regretted my decision to wear slacks and dress shoes almost immediately. There was a thin layer of frost on the stairs, and as we rose they only became more slippery.

"Try doing it in velvet Mary Janes. I swear, if I die, I'm going to be so mad at you." Livvie huffed up another set of stairs.

"As if I would let anything happen to you. Would be a bloody waste of redemption, wouldn't you say?" I was sure I was suffering far more. In addition to climbing, I was also pushing Livvie along to help her up the stairs.

"Bloody? I've never heard you say that before." She laughed. "And while I appreciate the chivalry, I'm pretty sure the redemption is for you."

"It's a common expression. Also—" I reached out to steady Livvie after she slipped on one of the stairs. "You okay?"

"Yeah, I'm okay. But seriously, James, can we *please* take the elevator once we get to the first platform? It's over a thousand stairs to the very top." She wrapped her arms around my neck as she caught her breath. Her forehead was a little sweaty and her cheeks were red from the cold. "Please?" She placed soft kisses on my cold cheek. "I'm begging." I laughed as I took in the sight of her mischievous smile and raised eyebrow.

"I suppose," I mumbled. I *really* did not want to get into that damn lift. I ride them very seldom and only while alone.

The first time I rode a lift was a few years after coming to live with Rafiq. He had business in Karachi and took me along. I must have been about sixteen or so. Rafiq didn't warn me the damnable contraption would move, and when I got out of the moving box of death I vomited in the lobby. Not only did I not get to accompany him into his meeting, but he made me ride the lift up and down the entire time he was gone. It took me about seven or eight trips and a threat of bodily harm from a security guard before I stopped yelling as the lift traveled between floors.

"You're the best boyfriend ever. You let me ride in elevators and everything." Livvie laughed somewhat maniacally.

"Laugh it up, Pet. It'll be *hilarious* when we get stuck and the smell of unclean tourist is invading your nostrils." Livvie only laughed harder as we continued our trek up the stairs.

"Don't worry, Sexy. I'll protect you." She turned and gave me a wink. Livvie was slowly picking up on some of my mannerisms and though I wouldn't admit it, it always made me feel... content.

"Good. I'll be the one trying to pry the doors open with my bare hands."

***

"God! I think tomorrow I'm going to wear slippers all day. My feet are *killing* me." Livvie hobbled toward the desk chair in our room and immediately reached for the strap holding her shoe in place.

"It was your idea to walk everywhere." I laughed as I poked fun at her. "Now you'll have blisters to commemorate our trip to Paris. You can tell Claudia all about the Parisian band-aids I purchased for you in the lobby." I mockingly switched to her vernacular. "She'll be *so jealous*." I winced as I kicked off my shoes. Livvie glared.

"I just hope she'll be able to hear me over the sound of her own laughter when I tell her how you yelled at that teenager and his girlfriend on the elevator."

"They were jumping up and down! Shaking the whole thing. They're lucky all I did was yell." I pulled up a chair in front of Livvie and reached for one of her feet. I was tempted to tip her over to stop her belly laughing.

Her laughter turned into a long keening moan as I rubbed her foot with both hands.

"Oh! I will love you forever if you don't stop."

A strange pang rippled through my chest. I ignored it. If Livvie loved me, she wasn't in any rush to let me know and I hadn't brought up my feelings for her since Thanksgiving. We were taking things slow and getting to know each other. We'd discussed it at length. Regardless, the words stirred me. The void yawned as if waking from a nap.

"This isn't chivalry," I countered. "I fully expect you to return the favor when I'm done. Also, I think a good back massage is in order. My muscles are tense after having been locked up tight during our gradual and torturous ascension."

Livvie smiled with her eyes closed.

"I love the way you say things."

She was thoroughly lost to my ministrations. Her lack of tactful word choice didn't even occur to her, and I suppose it made it that much easier to forgive. I knew that though she might not love me, she cared for me a great deal and would never hurt me on purpose.

Livvie continued, "I get a foot massage *and* the chance to rub you down? I really am the luckiest girl in Paris. Do you even notice how women look at you, Caleb? James. Whatever. You're just... you're fucking beautiful is what you are."

"Handsome. I'm handsome. And no, I don't notice. I'm too busy looking at you. Or using my carefully cultivated death-stare to threaten any man stupid enough to set eyes on you." I smiled at the contented sigh this elicited from Livvie.

"Yes, you definitely have a way with words. You should be a writer; you're certainly screwed up enough for the job."

"Aren't you the writer?"

Livvie opened her eyes and sat up. There was a brief moment when I perceived she was nervous, but it quickly faded. She was all flirty smiles when she spoke.

"Not really. It's not like anyone reads my stuff. It's all just on my laptop."

"Not true. Claudia has apparently read your work. I don't know if you know this, but I read. I could take a look if you'd like. Claudia seems to think it isn't to be missed."

Livvie slowly removed her foot from my lap and straddled me in my seat.

"What? You can read? I'm shocked!" She kissed me on the lips briefly.

"You're trying to distract me," I said, unimpressed.

"I am not. I'm just eager to give you that massage." She rubbed my shoulders and I groaned. "Will there be some sort of oil involved? The idea of sliding my hands all over you is really appealing. I could take off all my clothes if you'd like." She pressed her thumbs into my neck and ground her hips against me. I felt her breath as she whispered in my ear. "I'll even do the front."

"I won't forget about this," I said half-heartedly.

In all honesty, the only thing I was truly thinking about was slippery Livvie and how easy it would be to slide into her. Some days it seemed as though the only time I felt firmly connected to her was when I was literally inside her. I could imagine myself as her Prince Charming. I was not a monster. I was worthy. My heart was not an empty husk—it was engorged with blood and feeling.

"Hey," Livvie whispered against my mouth. "Where'd you go, Sexy?" She was worried. I could hear it in her voice and memories threatened to invade. I hated how familiar her worry was to me. I made eye contact with her.

"I'm here, exactly where I want to be."

She smiled.

"Me too." She kissed me slowly, passionately, and inherent within the press of lips there was an undercurrent of gratitude. It was difficult for me to accept given our circumstances, but the void consumed it nonetheless. It had the gall to demand more.

"Tell me you're mine, Livvie." The past intruded.

"I'm yours, Caleb." Her lips traveled across the side of my face and down my neck. Our attentions had gone from slow and passionate to fast and hungry. She sucked the flesh of my neck into her mouth, marking me. I already bore her scratches on my back. "And you're mine. Only mine."

I hated where Livvie and I had started. I loathed that I had ever wounded such an incredible person. However, the past was not without its comforts. It had been a time when I labored under the illusion of purpose and strength. Livvie unabashedly proclaimed her love for me and I held all the power. For all the horrors of my past, I took comfort in my understanding of the darkness in my soul. Livvie had let in the light and it blinded me. I groped for purchase within my new world. With Livvie at my side, I clung to her, powerless and oft times petrified. Moments like the one in which we found ourselves were sweet succor.

I undid the three tiny pearl buttons at Livvie's nape with care before I forcefully pulled the zipper along the back. She made a startled but eager sound against my neck. I spread the fabric and let it slide down her arms, pinning them to her sides. Livvie whimpered as she writhed against me. Her hips made little thrusts as she chased her pleasure.

I put my mouth against her collarbone and sucked. I had left my own marks on Livvie: I'd scraped my teeth along her hipbones. I'd left my handprint on her ass. There was a bruise near her nipple where I'd pinched her while she came. Her pussy still had my come in it from the night before. What more did I need? What more did I deserve?

"You make me feel so good," Livvie panted. Her knees dug into my hips and her hands tugged at my shirt in search of more contact. The long line of her throat, naked shoulders, and exposed cleavage were offered up to my mouth freely while Livvie's head was tossed back. I let my lips brush against the purple mark I'd left on her collarbone.

"Only good? I must not be trying near hard enough."

"Mmm... try harder then."

I gripped her hips and ground her down hard against my erection. She pulled her arms free of her dress and wrapped them around my neck as she attempted to ride me. I canted her hips back and held her in place, feasting on her hungry little sounds.

"Again with that mouth. So saucy."

"Caleb," she purred. "Stop fucking around. You know what I want."

I grinned.

"And what would that be?"

"You. Inside me."

My cock gave a little leap of excitement.

"You want to feel me?" I put my hand beneath her dress, skimming the sensitive flesh of her thighs where her stockings squeezed. I decided I would buy her garters, like a French girl would wear. I continued my exploration, lifting the trim of her lacy panties so I could graze her with my fingertips.

"Yes... please." I heard Livvie swallow. Her hips tried to guide my fingers. My finger pulled the scrap of fabric forward. Her panties were damp where her pussy had rested.

"Do you really think you deserve it? Am I the sort of man who appreciates a saucy mouth?" A memory: *I like your saucy little mouth. I don't want to hurt it.*

"I—" She pressed forward, cunt seeking. "I hope so."

I touched her with the back of my fingers.

"I do." I whispered and took her mouth, both of them, at the same time. She shuddered. I pumped my fingers into her heat as I collected her moans in my mouth. Livvie's pleasure was short lived. I withdrew my fingers slowly.

"But it doesn't mean you get to speak to me however you'd like."

She frowned.

"Caleb." I pressed my wet fingers to her mouth. She pulled back. She was shocked and a little disgusted. She'd licked her lip before she thought about it.

I brought her mouth to mine and licked her lips until she opened to me again. I liked the taste of pussy in her mouth. It drove me wild with lust. A familiar part of me enjoyed her horror and always would. I felt like myself. I felt powerful.

I pulled away from the kiss. I stood, carried Livvie toward the bed, and tossed her on it.

"Turn around and lie flat on the bed. I want to fuck you." Livvie sat, chest heaving, with her rumpled dress pooled around her waist. She reached for it, to take it off I assumed. "I didn't tell you to take it off," I snapped. Fear ignited behind her eyes and quickly burned down to an ember.

"Yes, Caleb," she whispered. Slowly, she turned and crawled toward the top of the bed. Once there, she lifted her dress to uncover her panties. The lacy fabric didn't cover her completely—it left the bottom of her cheeks exposed and framed her ass. She made eye contact, caught me looking. She smiled coyly and finally lay down on the bed.

"Yes, I like what I see. I would have thought that much was obvious by now." I palmed her ass with a loud smack. "No need to be smug." I reached for her panties and slid them down her legs. I stood up to remove my belt.

Livvie visibly tensed. Her hands fisted in the comforter. To her credit, she didn't move. She didn't turn to see what I was doing. She didn't ask what I was up to. She simply waited. Patient. Trusting. *Submissive.*

I was tempted to swat her with my belt. I pictured her gasping in surprise, her cheeks flexing and red. I imagined the way she would struggle to remain still. I visualized the raised welts my belt would leave. Another mark. Another brand. Another claim. My fist tightened on my belt. I let it go. I didn't want to remind her any more than I already had.

I undressed slowly. I took the time to hang my pants in the wardrobe. I set my other clothes aside to be sent in for washing. I watched Livvie the entire time, letting my lust build with every minute she patiently waited for me to return.

Or issue a command.

I riffled through the luggage to retrieve a bottle of oil I'd brought. I really did want that damn massage, but it could wait. I had different plans. I let my mouth nip and lick the backs of Livvie's legs on my way back up to her sexy ass. She trembled. A small squeak escaped her lips when I drizzled the oil in her cleft.

"Is this okay?" I asked. I didn't need an answer to my question. I simply enjoyed listening to her answer. She was slow to acquiesce. It wasn't until I rubbed the oil into her crack with the head of my cock that her lips opened.

"Y-y-yes?" I rubbed harder. "Oh… wait… please…" Livvie propped herself up on her elbows and tried to drag her body higher up on the bed. She couldn't. She was pinned beneath me.

"Shhh." I held her elbows and urged her back down. "Do you trust me, Kitten?" I unfastened her bra and massaged the red marks it had left. She liked that. "Do you believe me when I tell you I wouldn't hurt you? Not like before. Not ever." My thumbs pressed on either side of her spine between her shoulders and pressed forward to the base of her neck. Livvie sighed.

"Yes. I trust you." Her mouth went slack and her muscles loosened beneath my hands. "Just... be gentle."

I sported a sad smile Livvie couldn't see. The first time she'd said those words to me, she'd thought I was about to make love to her. Instead, she'd told me she loved me and I'd been cruel. I wouldn't make the same mistake.

I settled the length of my body on top of her. I kissed her shoulder.

"I promise, Kitten. I'll stop if you don't want it." I pressed my cock against her. "Spread your legs." There was no hesitation this time. Livvie's thighs spread on either side of me in invitation.

I watched the side of her face intently as I moved my hips. My dick was slippery. I knew she could feel the heat and weight of it sliding between her cheeks. Penetration could not happen, and having removed the threat of it, I knew the temptation would be planted.

Livvie's eyes were closed, only opening occasionally when accompanied by a shy moan. Her teeth worried at her lip and already her fingers were near her mouth. The pink stain of arousal painted her cheek.

I kissed her cheek, the back of her neck, her shoulder—faint little kisses that offered comfort but did nothing to soothe the heat of arousal. I wanted her delirious with desire. I wanted her pulsing with lust. I wanted her to beg.

I adjusted my angle and for the first time let the tip brush against her opening. It was an implicit suggestion, but only that. I wanted her to crave my domination as much as I desired her submission.

Triumph!

Livvie let out a pleading sound. Her hips made little thrusts before she could help it. I went back to rocking against her. I treasured Livvie's sigh of disappointment, the way she forced her hips to stop moving.

"Tell me what you want," I said hotly in her ear.

She frowned, resisting.

I pulled my hips back and brushed her hole with an oiled finger. I pressed inside slowly, only to the first knuckle. Livvie was moaning loudly. I withdrew.

"Tell me."

"Please, Caleb." She lifted tail.

"Tell me." I held the tip of my cock against her and pushed gently.

"Oh god!" She fisted the sheets and arched her back. "Please, Caleb. I *need* you."

That was certainly good enough for me. However, having suddenly gained the submission I desired, I wondered if I was perhaps wrong to accept.

I kissed Livvie's shoulder.

"Thank you for that. I know I'm a difficult man to trust." My fingers found her wet flesh and slipped inside. It was familiar territory. It did not require me to be overly gentle or careful. It did not require her to bend her will to mine. It was *safe*.

Livvie hissed in arousal. Her hips moved as much as they were able beneath my weight.

"What are you doing?" Her voice carried on little more than breath.

I curved my fingers downward, pressing against the front of her inner walls. I knew I could make her come that way.

"I thought it was obvious. First, I'm going to make you come and then I'm going to fuck you until you do it again. And maybe once more after that."

119

She whimpered. I lived for that sound.

"But... I thought... oh god... right there." A series of moans and incoherent begging filled the small, intimate space between Livvie's mouth and my ears. A wet rush escaped around my buried fingers. Livvie's body was rigid, hijacked by her orgasm. And then she went limp. I slowly withdrew my fingers. I was eager to replace them.

"No, Caleb," she murmured into the bedding. "Not like that."

"Not like what?"

"I know what you want."

"I don't want to hurt you."

"I want it to hurt," she whispered.

Her hair was matted to her forehead. Her body was flushed, and her eyes were closed. She didn't acknowledge my tense reaction. She didn't open her eyes to take in the moment. She seemed afloat in her bliss despite asking me to hurt her. *Who the hell are you?*

"You *want* me to hurt you?" I whispered.

She was quiet for a moment.

"I trust you, Caleb."

"But..."

"Shhh," she cooed. "Don't analyze it. Just do it."

With more than a small amount of trepidation, I did. I pressed into her ass in miniscule degrees. I could hear her breathing, deep breaths, in and out. She was willing me into her body through her submission. She kept herself open and ready.

My heart beat with enough force to leave a bruise in my chest. I didn't understand. She wanted me to change. She wanted someone different. Didn't she? Why was she baiting me? Part of me didn't care. I wanted it too much to care. I focused on my shallow thrusts. I focused on the pressure surrounding me and the dull scrape of every hard-earned inch I buried.

Livvie whimpered. It was a sound born of pain. I held myself perfectly still.

"More," she whispered. I obeyed.

There were tears in her eyes by the time I was fully inside. I was almost afraid to move, but equally as determined to take what Livvie had so boldly offered. My mind was befuddled—my body was not.

"Last chance," I said. I pressed my lips to her cheek and they came away wet. I licked my lips to ingest her tears. I had tasted her sadness. I had tasted her joy. I wondered what kind of tears I tasted in that moment.

"*Please,*" and her rocking hips were her response.

I was so tangled up inside, it was a relief to let my body take over. I let myself fall: into a rhythm, into the void, into Livvie. I let her moans, whimpers, and cries into my ears. I answered them with groans, grunts, and hisses of breath. As my pace increased, the sound of our bodies slamming together joined in the chorus.

Livvie writhed beneath me. Sometimes she urged me deeper, harder, and faster. Other times, her sounds and movements begged me to go slower and pull back. There was no stop. Stop was unacceptable to us both.

When I couldn't take the heat, I pulled Livvie up onto her knees. She pushed back against me, burying me inside. She cried out, coming and riding me hard. My world tilted on its axis. *Mine!*

"I'm going to come," I warned.

Livvie was panting hard.

"Tell me you love me," she said.

"You first!" I yelled and spilled inside her.

We didn't discuss any of it afterward. Neither of us was willing to cede any further emotional territory.

CHAPTER TEN

By the time early January reared its head, Livvie and I were starting to settle into being a couple. Granted, we weren't your average couple, but we were getting comfortable with who we were. The nightmares became less frequent and we attacked each other less often. Livvie let me put it in her ass sometimes (grin).

Naturally, I had to try my best to fuck it all up.

Okay, before I even go on, please let me say I am not proud of what I did next. I was bored and insatiably curious. Also, in case you haven't noticed, I'm not your typical boyfriend material.

It was the first time I'd ever been in Livvie's apartment alone. She had classes during the day but didn't have to work in the evening. She asked if I'd be there when she came home and I said yes because it beat being in my hotel room.

The sun flooded Livvie's apartment. I lay in her bed, smothered in throw pillows of various colors and shapes (Seriously ladies, what the fuck with all the pillows?). I felt especially dirty jerking off in her frilly bed. I was sure to wipe up my come with a fuzzy pink pillow. I hoped it would prompt Livvie to throw the damn thing away.

Afterward, I took a shower, made myself a bowl of Cocoa Puffs, and perused the stack of movies Livvie had rented and left on the coffee table. I'd never been the type of man who liked to eat cereal, let alone kid cereal, but Livvie loved the stuff and it was often the only thing I could find in her kitchen. I knew she could cook when she wanted to, but it seemed the mood rarely struck her. Some nights we ate cereal for dinner.

I decided not to watch the movies without Livvie since she seemed to enjoy regaling me with random movie factoids as we watched. I made the mistake of asking why we were watching "Episode IV" instead of starting from the beginning, and what followed was a diatribe about George Lucas and how he ruined *Star Wars* when he released three prequels. I didn't much care, but I enjoyed watching Livvie rant about things that weren't me. What I didn't much enjoy was the way she stared at me the entire time I watched the movie to gauge my response during "awesome" scenes.

As I sat on the couch eating my cereal, my eyes landed on Livvie's laptop. It was just sitting on the coffee table—daring me! Livvie was on the thing whenever she had time. I desperately wanted to know what Livvie had been writing and why she was keeping it from me. I remembered the way Livvie had snapped at Claudia to be quiet. Then the way she'd avoided the topic in Paris. It only made me more curious. I determined fairly quickly it had to be about me, us, or better—her.

I shoveled the remainder of my cereal into my mouth and set the bowl on the table. I scooped up the laptop and opened it. A smile curved my lips when I saw her screensaver. It was a picture of me asleep on her couch on Thanksgiving. I was wearing pants, but the photograph focused on my face and naked chest. *What a little pervert, taking pictures of me while I'm helpless.*

I was prompted for a password. Why did she need a password? Didn't she trust me? I hope you're smiling, because I know I am.

Anyway, it took me the better part of the morning, but I finally gained access to Livvie's laptop. Her password gave me mixed emotions: Survival. If you're horrified, please consider that I was fully aware Livvie would discover what I'd done. I wasn't trying to hide my actions. I just wanted to know what the hell was on her laptop and why she chose to keep it from me.

There was a fleeting moment when I considered I might be opening Pandora's box, but it really was fleeting. I make it my business to know what's going on around me, and it has saved my ass more than once.

Livvie is very systematic. Her desktop was organized into a series of folders: FLM101, ENG202, HIS152, ART102, School Plan, and most alluring, Captive. One guess as to which folder I opened first? No! Not film.

There were several different documents inside the folder: Caleb, Reed, Sloan, FBI procedures, Mexico, East, Stockholm Syn, Human Traffick, Captive_D1_R2. My fingers began to shake as I hovered over each file. I wondered what I would discover. I wondered if I could process what I'd find. I wondered if I would feel different toward Livvie once I read them. If she was betraying me in some way, did I want to know? I knew already there would be no going back. Ignorance had never served me well.

I tested the waters by opening the document labeled "Sloan". It contained a description of her appearance and a list of her mannerisms. I found Sloan interesting in a strange sort of way (free-form knitting and interpretive taxidermy? What?). I immediately moved on to the file on Reed.

> *Height: 6'2" Weight: 195? Desc: Pitch black hair that's a little too long (surprising because of his job and his obvious anal retentiveness). It curls a little around his ears and the nape of his neck. His eyes are dark and expressive due to his dark brows. Clean shaven (very meticulously groomed aside from the hair). His lips (mmmmm). His mouth is warm and he tastes*

like coffee and mints. Bit of an angry shit when you kiss him unexpectedly (ha!).

Rage hit me fast and hard. Why had she kissed him? What had she really been up to when Reed had come to "check on her"?

I had to stop reading and take a few deep breaths. Livvie wouldn't betray me. Would she? She obviously hadn't turned me in. I forced myself to keep reading.

Livvie went on to describe Reed as good looking and sharp witted. I'm fucking good looking and sharp witted! I bet Reed only speaks one language. I'm sharp witted in five!

I moved on to my file. Surely, it had to read better than the one she had on Reed. I recalled Livvie telling me in Mexico that she hoped to write a book one day. She'd also told me the first rule of writing was to write what you know. The thought filled me with foreboding.

The document was longer than the previous two— about three pages. She'd managed a great deal of detail. The description calmed me somewhat. Livvie was very flattering, except I felt she had transformed me from a person into a character, and I wasn't sure how I felt about being picked apart.

Height: 6'4" Weight: 210? Desc: blond hair, Caribbean blue eyes. A full mouth made for kissing. He has a canine tooth that is a bit sharp and slightly out of line with all of this other perfect teeth (the first time I saw him smile). Muscular, but lean—not bulky or overly muscled. His skin is tan from the sun, not a machine. He has almost invisible blond hair everywhere (kissing his back, they stood on end—super soft).

Mannerisms: Caleb always seems to think something is funny or amusing (that ridiculous smirk). His eyes can be beautiful or fucking terrifying (peaceful waters v. dark murky water). His mouth gets tense when he's pissed and trying not to show it. He scowls a lot and sometimes he does it while he's smiling, which usually means he's about to do something especially cruel (that first whipping).

Livvie's character profile went on and on about me. She wrote down pieces of things she remembered about me. She even went on to describe my dick, what I looked like when I came, and the way I laughed. Had Claudia read these notes? I knew she'd read at least part of Livvie's story. What the fuck could she possibly have been thinking? I resented taking instant notice of how tight my lips were as I bit down on the tip of my tongue to help calm me down. I laughed bitterly.

I finally opened *Captive*.

Prologue:

 This is not a romance. Romances are filled with valiant men and simpering damsels in distress. Romances have heroes worthy of the title. They slay dragons and climb towers to rescue beautiful princesses they immediately marry and impregnate. Romances end with a happily ever after. This is not a romance.

 This is a love story. The characters are flawed to the point of being broken. The hero is beautiful, but ugly in ways that defy the ordinary imagination. The heroine isn't trapped in a tower, but a dark and lonely room. There is no prince coming to save her. While love blooms and thrives, there is no happily ever after. Love does not always begin or end the way we wish it would.

 A love story can happen to anyone. This one happened to me.

The words stirred something inside me. There wasn't a doubt in my mind. Livvie was writing a book about us. Our story was not romance. I was not worthy of being called a hero. I was beautiful on the outside and hideous on the inside. We... didn't have a happily ever after.

I swallowed hard. I swallowed a few times.

I'd come too far to stop. I kept reading:

I'm hurrying down the sidewalk, trying to get away from the sinister man in the car behind me, when I look up and see him. Perhaps it's his easy stride, or the way his gaze sweeps past me instead of over me, but for whatever reason, he seems safe. I throw my arms about his waist and whisper, "Just play along, okay?"

He does, and I'm surprised when his arms wrap around me. The moment of danger seems to pass very quickly, but for some reason I don't want to let go. I feel safe in these arms, and I've never really felt safe before. And he smells good, he smells the way I imagine a man should smell—like crisp, clean soap, and warm skin, and a light sweat. I think I'm taking too long to let go, so I release him as though he's burned me. Then I stare up and acknowledge the angel in front of me. My knees almost buckle.

He is the most beautiful thing I have ever seen. That includes puppies, babies, rainbows, sunsets, and sunrises. I can't even call him a man—men don't look this good. His skin is beautifully tanned, as if the sun itself took the time to kiss his skin to perfection. His muscled forearms are dusted with the same golden hair of his head. And his eyes mimic the blue-green of the Caribbean Sea I've only seen on movie posters.

He smiles, and I can't help but smile, too. I'm a puppet. He pulls my strings. His smile reveals his beautiful white teeth, but also his sharp canine on the left side. His teeth aren't per-

127

fect, and the small imperfection seems to make him more beautiful.

He's saying something to me, something about another girl, but I refuse to listen.

It was the first time we'd met. She'd felt safe in my arms, never guessing, never knowing what I was about to do to her. Even knowing all the things that happened afterward, the fact we were having a relationship, I felt sick to my stomach over her words. Her choice of phrases made her youth obvious. She'd compared me to puppies, babies, and rainbows. So young and naïve—I'd ruined that.

Livvie's first draft looked nothing like what you've read. She didn't have my perspective. She didn't have the knowledge of my thoughts or the things that were in play during those first encounters. The picture she painted was of a sad, lonely girl trapped in a room at the hands of a sadistic monster who cared nothing for her well-being. This was Livvie's recollection of me.

I read about her kidnapping, living every moment of her fear with her and feeling rage when she talked about Jair slapping her unconscious. It was beyond surreal to read about Livvie's first impressions of my cold and detached voice as she lay bound and blind in Felipe's house. She'd thought I was going to rape and kill her. I suppose I knew those things then, but I didn't care and that was the worst part. I remembered I hadn't cared. That was the truth about the man I was.

I was a glutton for punishment and I kept reading. To my surprise, I found erotic undertones. While I remembered the moments vividly and with a certain sick fondness, reading them from her point of view was like a knife twisting in my gut. I wasn't sure if the Livvie I had come to know was honestly the Livvie she had been. Perhaps I had simply altered her to suit me.

I wondered if Livvie had been someone else, a different girl as I had once suggested, if I would have gone through with it and sold her to Vladek. I wondered if Livvie had never gotten away from me, never suffered the encounter with the bikers, if I might have taken this beautiful woman and ruined her. In those moments, I would have done anything to unmake the words in front of me. I didn't want them to exist. I didn't want them to be true. With all that I was, I longed to go back to that first day I had met Livvie and make different choices. Yet there was the nagging voice in my head reminding me how far back I'd have to go to undo my mistakes. I would have to go back to the night Narweh beat me and give up my fight to live.

Where would Livvie be in her life if I had just died?

Where would all of the women I had made suffer be? I'd been too late to save Pia Kumar. I'd buried her masters alive next to her so that she might be able to hear their screams.

I had to look away from the screen. I had to set the laptop down and walk onto the balcony for air. My chest felt heavy.

It was no wonder she couldn't say she loved me. What right did I have to love?

I went inside and wrote her a note.

I read your book. I know you'll be furious and you have a right. I realize you'll want to scream at me and you have a right to that as well, but I have to be honest and tell you I'm not sure I can take it just yet. I'll be at the hotel for a few days. I need to think.

Yours,
Caleb

p.s. I'm sorry for all of it.

I gathered up what meager belongings I had in Livvie's apartment and locked the door behind me when I left. I was numb and unsure what to do next.

I could barely drive. My attention wasn't focused on the road, but on Livvie. Why had she let me stay with her? After all the things I had put her through, I couldn't imagine her reasons for inviting me back into her life. Perhaps it was only that she feared me. Perhaps she only wanted to keep me close and keep an eye on me. It was the smart thing to do. It's what I would do.

I hated how weak my feelings for her had made me. I was not a sniveling child. I hated the way I felt empty when she wasn't around. I loathed waiting in my hotel room for her to get out of school or off work. I thought of her as mine. She was mine, and yet I couldn't touch her where it mattered. I couldn't touch her heart and force her to give me the things I had stupidly come to need. For a moment… I hated her. I hated loving her.

I'd meant to return to my hotel, but my thoughts took me elsewhere. I'd seen the gym a few times and had even considered going inside, but I ultimately decided against it. I was a violent person. I didn't think it was a good idea to be around violence. I had apparently changed my mind. My violence needed to be let out.

I parked the vehicle and went inside. I was immediately assaulted by the smell of male sweat. The room practically teemed with body odor. There was no air conditioning, or escalators, or walls lined with treadmills and circuit training machines. This was a real gym. This was a place where men went to commune with the beast that lives in all of us.

Adrenaline found me at last. My heart pounded with it, my fists clenched, my muscles yawned and flexed. I was practically lusting for a fight. I searched the room for someone who might be willing and able to take me on.

"Can I sign you up?" someone asked in Spanish. I turned and glared at the man behind me. He wasn't particularly tall, but he carried himself with extreme confidence. He was perhaps a little younger than me too, and I thought that added to his demeanor. I took my measure slowly and decided the man was likely a martial artist of some kind—his legs looked capable of snapping bones.

"I'd like to fight," I said as calmly as I was able. I must not have been very successful in portraying calm because he eyed me somewhat suspiciously.

"English? Okay. I speak little bit. You need..." He struggled for a word but ended up tugging on his clothes.

"I didn't bring any," I said. "I don't need any. Just like this." I swept my hand across my t-shirt and jeans. I didn't bother explaining I could speak Spanish. I wasn't in the mood for conversation. He smiled and shook his head.

"Fighter? What style?" He walked back toward the front door and into a room on the left. I assumed it was the office. I stepped inside, somewhat annoyed I couldn't just jump into the action.

"I'm trained." Rafiq had been a military officer and had given me quite the education. One of my favorite memories was the day I'd finally bested him in hand to hand. He'd taken a big risk teaching me all that he did. Without him I'd have been an illiterate, defenseless whore. It was ironic that the very skills he'd taught me had aided in his demise.

The man at the desk rolled his eyes and muttered about me in Spanish. He thought I was an idiot who'd come to get his ass kicked. He seemed amused by the idea. He grabbed some papers from a printer behind him and placed them in front of me.

"Please to write all your information and sign the bottom. Need identification and money for membership."

I filled in the necessary information and took out all the cash in my wallet. It was enough to cover my membership for three months. The man at the desk seemed pleased with my payment and stood to shake my hand.

"Carlos."

Seeing no reason to make a new enemy, I shook his hand and tried out my name.

"James." I dropped my hand and looked toward the ring. "Can I fight now?"

Carlos shook his head, somewhat exasperated.

"Okay. You fight." He walked beyond me and I followed him toward the ring. He called out to a nearby fighter. I listened while he informed the man of my intentions. The fighter sized me up and smirked before he informed Carlos he was willing to take me on. Neither of them seemed to think I had any talent.

I paid them little mind as I removed my socks, shoes, and shirt. I didn't care how the fight was going to go. I only cared about hitting. I accepted the ill-fitting mouth guard handed to me and put it in my mouth. I also took heed and wore the required headgear.

Within minutes, I stood in the ring across from Fernando. I thought we were fairly matched. He was a touch shorter than me, but his muscles were bulkier and more defined. I knew his fighting style involved the use of his legs as he stretched them, bending his feet toward his ass.

I rolled my head and shoulders, shaking my arms out. I bounced on the balls of my feet, warming my muscles as much as I could in the short span of time I'd given myself to prepare. I held no illusions about not getting hit. In fact, I craved the blows that would soon land on me. I knew they would incense me. I knew they would trigger the rage I'd been keeping locked inside. I knew once the rage took over, all thoughts of Livvie would cease. I knew the pain inside would yield to the pain on the outside.

Carlos called us toward the center and went over the rules for my benefit: No gouging, biting, breaking of bones, hits to the groin, head-butting, or fighting after the bell. There were more rules than I was used to, but then again I'd never fought anyone but Rafiq for fun. Even then, I was learning survival. Implicit in the rules, but not necessary for anyone but me, was one more rule: No killing.

Fernando and I nodded at one another and took one or two steps back from the center. Carlos left the ring and took a position not far away. He rang the bell. The man opposite me was not eager. Despite the smirk and over-confidence he displayed, he took the time to circle the ring and gauge my strengths. I did the same.

It erupted quickly. For all that I was expecting a kick from his powerful legs, I was caught off guard when he simply rushed me with the full force of his body. He lifted me and threw my back into the corner. A knee came up and landed on my ribs. My breath left me in a rush.

My hands free, I joined them together and hit him in the junction between neck and shoulder. He took a step back and I landed another blow in the same spot before I had enough room to lift my right leg and push him back.

He smiled and made a motion with his upraised hands: Come on.

He'd winded me and I had barely done anything to convince him I was a worthy opponent. It was a situation I intended to remedy quickly. I came at him with a series of kicks that he met easily enough. I came at him with so many kicks he diverted his attention from my hands and I made my move. I punched him in the side of the neck with my left, stepped in, and sent an elbow to his temple with my right. He lost enough of his balance I was able to hook one of his legs and push him to the mat.

Fernando was a skilled fighter and the attack did not daze him for long. He quickly rolled, catching me with his powerful legs and flinging me to the mat. His foot came up and his heel landed on my back with impressive force. The gym seemed to come to life in those moments as others began to gather around the ring. They cheered for Fernando.

On the mat, we grappled, each of us avoiding an arm around the neck or an arm grab that would undoubtedly lead to a painful submission hold. The bell rang before either of us was willing to surrender our position.

"Separate!" called Carlos. I kicked Fernando off of me and scrambled to my feet. We stared at one another and heaved for breath. Carlos was laughing and remarked that I had more fight than he thought.

Fernando told me not to get too excited. He'd been taking it easy on me but was ready to kick my ass just as soon as Carlos rung the bell.

I took off my headgear and threw it outside the ring. Mimicking Fernando's hand gesture from earlier, I raised my hands and told him to kick my ass if he thought he could. Everyone seemed pleasantly surprised by my ability to speak Spanish. Everyone except Fernando. He removed his own headgear and tossed it. Carlos rang the bell.

Fernando rushed again, but I was ready this time. I waited until he was within arm's reach and used his momentum against him. I stepped to the side, caught his neck with my arm and jumped on his back. We went down with a loud thud as I rode Fernando to the ground. With my knees firmly planted in his sides, I went to work punching Fernando in the face before he covered himself. My hands throbbed with pain after colliding with bone.

Fernando rolled, knocking me to the side, and delivered a backward kick that landed between my shoulder blades. I cried out, my hands scrambling for purchase on the other man's sweaty flesh. Wearing jeans had been a mistake. The fabric trapped me. Two more kicks landed on my back and I saw spots.

The fight had gone from a sparring match to an earnest struggle. Fernando scrambled to get on my back, his arms trying to wind their way around my neck. I kept my arm up to protect my windpipe.

A familiar feeling spread throughout my body. Suddenly, the only thing that mattered was winning. A fist collided with the side of my face and my teeth bit down hard on the mouth guard. I could taste blood in my mouth.

"You can't kill me, Khoya. *I'm a god here."*

I gritted my teeth and pushed with all my strength on the arm attempting to circle my neck. Fernando's arm trembled and eventually he was forced to readjust his position on my back. The bell rang and Carlos yelled for us to separate, but neither of us listened. I refused to be saved by the bell for a second time.

I pushed myself up with my arms, exposing my neck to Fernando in a way he couldn't resist. As he wrapped his arm around my neck, his face pressed to the side of my own, I reached behind his head with one arm and grasped my other hand. I squeezed. Fernando grunted into my ear. I crushed his windpipe with my shoulder as I pressed him from behind.

With each of us having the other by the throat, it became a test of endurance. Fernando's position was better than mine, but he was used to fighting for sport. I was accustomed to fighting to live. I squeezed until my shoulders burned. I had run out of oxygen long ago and black spots invaded my vision. But I held on. I held on until I felt Fernando sag against me, only seconds before I blacked out.

I was jolted into consciousness by a forceful slap and cold water being splashed on my face. Carlos' angry glare was all I needed to realize what had happened. I looked beyond him to watch as another man treated Fernando to the same. He sat up with a cough and rubbed at his neck.

"I knew you were a troublemaker when you walked in," Carlos said in Spanish. "Get dressed and get the fuck out." He stood and tossed my shirt onto my chest. I pulled it on and stood as quickly as I was able.

"Good fight," I managed through a strained throat. "We'll do it again." Fernando managed to smile and nod as I turned to leave the ring.

I grabbed my socks and shoes and left without putting them on. The cold was bracing as I walked toward my car, but I didn't mind. It was the only thing keeping me upright. I knew I'd be bruised to hell in the morning. At last, something felt normal.

I managed to get back to the hotel before the first stirrings of bruised muscle, scraped flesh, and weary bones had me longing for the comfort of a hot bath. Slowly, I eased my body into the water. It stung viciously.

I put ice on my face. No one could accuse me of being pretty at that moment.

CHAPTER ELEVEN

I was sound asleep when I heard the pounding on the door. I moaned as I attempted to move all at once. The light coming in through the curtains told me it wasn't yet evening. Livvie hadn't waited long before coming to find me.

I decided further movement was ill advised. My throat was too sore to yell. A strange pinch occurred in my chest. I wanted to see Livvie, but I didn't want to fight with her.

> *Vivisected. It's the only word I can think of to describe how I'm feeling—vivisected. As though someone has cut me open with a scalpel, the pain not sinking in until the flesh begins to separate and my blood bubbles out. I can hear the crack as my ribs are flayed open. Slowly, my organs, wet and sticky, are pulled out of me one at a time. Until I am hollow. Hollow and yet, in excruciating pain—still alive. Still. Alive.*

As I lay unable or unwilling to move with Livvie pounding on my door, it occurred to me: *It's always going to hurt.* Yes, vivisected had been a very apt word to use. Loving Livvie was like allowing myself to be peeled open and hollowed out. She made me weak. She made me vulnerable. She made me ache and long and hope for all the things that could never be mine.

The door opened.

"Caleb?" Livvie called out. It was the first time she'd ever used the key I'd given her and I groaned at my own stupidity. That was another thing Livvie made me—stupid.

"I'm in here," I said. Getting choked until unconscious is hard on the vocal chords. I hated the way my heart knocked in my chest. I really wanted to see her. I wanted to tell her I was sorry. Shamefully, I wanted her to see me battered and use it to keep her from screaming at me.

She gasped when she saw me but didn't reach out to touch me.

"What did you do now? I mean, aside from invade my privacy and break my trust? It's been a busy day for you."

I let her words hang in the air between us. What could I say? Finally, she stepped closer and brushed her fingers across my cheek. I hissed.

"Serves you right," she snapped. Beneath the anger I heard concern. "What happened?"

"I picked a fight," I whispered. "You should see the other guy." I laughed and it hurt.

"Is—is the other guy alive?" she asked without inflection.

"Yes," I said just as coldly. "You would ask me, wouldn't you? I'm always killing people for petty reasons." I turned away from her. "If you came for a fight, don't bother. I surrender." I felt an intense pressure in my chest. "Just go."

"Do you really want me to go?" she asked. There was no emotion in her voice and it scared the fuck out me. *Please, don't go. Don't leave me.*

"If you're done with me," I said instead.

"Coward," she spat. "You'll take a beating. You'll face men with guns. You'll kill. But God forbid you have to swallow your goddamn pride and apologize for being a nosy little shit."

I sat up fast.

"You think I don't swallow my pride? Fuck you! All I've done for months is swallow my pride. I've apologized ad nauseum. I fuck you when you want to be fucked. I

139

play nice for your friends. I wait for you to come home because I have nothing more to do. You've become my whole life!

"Meanwhile, you're writing about me. You still see me as the man I was. You still see the killer—beautiful on the outside and hideous on the inside. Why are you with me? Why am I trying so hard to be someone else when all I'll ever be to you is the man who ruined your life? I follow you around like a love-sick bitch and every day I fight the urge to go back to what I know. There are days when I want to go back to being the person I was because that person couldn't love you. The man I was would *never* be this weak!"

I shouted through the pain in my throat and that, coupled with the emotion working its way to the surface, threatened to close off my airway. Livvie's face was a mask of indifference. It chilled my bones. How had she learned to be so cold? I knew the answer even as I asked the question.

"You love me?" she asked as she looked into my eyes. "When did you come to the realization? Was it when I told you I loved you and you said it was cute? Or maybe it was after I killed a man? Possibly when I begged you not to leave me at the border?

"Did you realize you loved me while I was alone in the hospital and weeping over you? When did you shout your love from the rooftops, Caleb? I couldn't hear you. I was too busy trying to fucking breathe without you. I was busy convincing everyone around me I wasn't crazy for defending my kidnapper. So, remind me. When did you say the words? I'll be sure to go back in time and comfort the broken girl you left in your wake. Your love can comfort her, because I'm not the same person anymore.

"I've learned to breathe without you. I've learned there's no one in this life I can trust. It isn't that you read my words. I don't care about that. I would have shown you eventually. It's the note you left. It's now. It's knowing that at any moment you're going to run off and leave me again. How can I tell you I love you? How could I survive it again?"

I was stunned into silence. Every cell in my body crawled with shame. Livvie was a survivor. She'd survived *me*. I realized then what I was witnessing was not indifference—it was pain. Livvie was in pain and it was my fault.

I didn't know what was happening, but it came on suddenly. My nose started running and I sniffled. I knew Livvie was watching me. I knew how ridiculous I must look, how weak and broken. I couldn't even care. I had nothing left to lose. I did my best to clear my throat before I spoke.

"I couldn't say it, Kitten. I'd just finished... I loved him." I felt my chest shaking.

"Who?" Livvie whispered. She was still so stoic.

"Rafiq," I said softly. Livvie sighed.

"Why, Caleb? You know what he did."

"Yes. I know what he did. I also know what he didn't do: He never touched me the way the others did." A part of me couldn't believe I was about to go into this with her. I'd read her story and it had me thinking of my own. I suppose I thought I owed her the other half of our tale. I needed her to know I hadn't cast her out without good reasons. "I was so young, Livvie. I was so powerless. Every day I was raped by someone. I was raped every day until I started to convince myself it wasn't rape. I let them touch me. I let them... fuck me. I smiled at the ones I saw more often than the others, imagining they must care for me. Why else would they come back to use me repeatedly?

"Eventually, I believed them. I believed them when they said they cared. I believed them when they promised to buy me from Narweh. I let myself hope that one day I would be free." I heard myself sob. The sound was far away, as though someone else were falling apart and not me. "It never happened. They never cared. They were never going to set me free. It was the hope they loved to toy with—my hope. I let it die.

"And then one day... Rafiq came. He picked me up, whipped and bloody. He took me home and nursed me. He fed me. He fed my body. He fed my mind. He fed my soul. He taught me how to do more than survive—he taught me how to *live*. And he never touched me.

"For years he took care of me. I didn't need hope anymore. I had something better. I had *purpose!* I loved him for that. And then..." I felt numb as I stared off into space. "I learned the truth."

My body shook as I recalled the night I murdered him.

"I wasn't anything, Livvie. I wasn't anything to him and he'd been *everything* to me. I would have died for him and the whole time... I was nothing." I finally looked at Livvie. Tears were on her cheeks. "But that's not the worst part. No, the worst part is that I meant to kill him before I knew the truth. It was the only way to set you free and I... I killed him, Livvie. I killed him and I buried him in Felipe's garden where his family will never find him. I buried the only person I thought I could trust. I loved him, and he turned out to be the person responsible for the most horrendous betrayal of my life.

"And then I realized I'd done the same to you. I'd beaten you. I'd raped you, and worse—I even made you like it. I fed you hope and I snatched it away. I made you love me! How could I tell you? I couldn't tell you, Livvie. I was confused. I was... *broken*. I'm *still* broken. I don't know who I am or what I want. All I know is that without you... without you, there's nothing. I'm nothing. Do you have any idea how terrifying that is for someone like me?"

My feelings toward her were on the tip of my tongue. I'd been holding the words in since the moment I had watched her walk out of my life, and if she'd turned around and looked at me for even a second, I wouldn't have been able to resist telling her then.

I love you.

I couldn't say it in Mexico. I had lost too much that day. I had lost my reality. What could I possibly understand about love when the only person I was sure I did love had lied to me for twelve years? Livvie had said she was mine. How could I be sure? Worse, what if it were true? What if she loved me and all I had to offer was a husk of a heart to love her with? How can anyone understand what love is without experiencing it? It would be like trying to describe color to a blind man. Some things you have to see for yourself. To understand love, you have to feel it for yourself.

It wasn't until Livvie walked away and I was truly alone in the world that I began to feel what love could be. It didn't come to me as it came to others; I had to find love as I had found everything else that defined me: through my suffering. The chasm Livvie's absence opened in me was a hungry void. It was alive, the void, and it would not be filled with vengeance. It was not soothed by my attempts to right my wrongs. It was not pleased by random women. It did not sleep, despite the amount of drink I imbibed to dull my senses.

There was only one thing the void wanted. Greedily tearing me apart, it asked for Livvie. It wanted my hopes, my dreams. It wanted my memories of her face. It wanted the laughter we had shared. "Mine," the void had decreed. Only Livvie could make me whole, and as soon as I had realized it, I couldn't stop looking for her. I'd become obsessed with knowing if she really loved me.

The first touch of Livvie's hand on my shoulder had me sobbing again. Love made me weak. I wished it would go away. Instead, it crushed me under its heel. I let Livvie push me back onto the bed. And when I heard her turn away, love made me beg.

"Please don't go. Don't leave me."

I felt her fingers running through my hair.

"I would never leave you, Caleb. I just wanted to get you some water."

"I don't want water."

"Scotch? Whiskey?"

"Just you."

There was a long pause.

"Okay."

I heard her undress before she slipped in behind me. She smelled like smoke. She hadn't had a cigarette since the first night I'd come to her apartment. I didn't say anything about it. She had her vises and I had mine. All that mattered to me was that Livvie was warm. And soft. Livvie was always warm and soft. She spoke softly in my ear.

"I'm scared too. You didn't come to the door and I thought: He left me again. Caleb, you can't *do that* to me."

Livvie kissed my shoulder, but I could feel her vibrating with anger.

"You're mad at me."

"Yes," she said. "But I guess... maybe I can't blame you. In the grand scheme of things, it's ridiculous to assume you *wouldn't* break into my laptop. To use your words: I know who you are and I know what you do." Livvie let out a short burst of laughter that quickly became a thoughtful sigh. "It must be hard on you, not having anyone to talk to about... *him*. I certainly don't care he's dead—he can rot in hell for all I care—but I never guessed how much you..." Livvie sighed and went silent.

"I don't expect you to care. I don't regret what I did. I just wanted you to know why I couldn't let you come with me. To be honest, I don't regret leaving you behind."

She tensed.

"Sorry you came back?"

I turned and pulled her into my arms. It wasn't her place to comfort me.

"No. I could never regret any amount of time with you. You're the best thing that's ever happened in my life. I just wish I could... be that for you." Her silence was nearly deafening. It was a confirmation.

"I... fuck. I'm so goddamn angry, Caleb. I don't know how to process everything sometimes. There's so much living inside me. *That's* what the writing is for, it helps me lay shit out and filter through my thoughts." She propped herself up on her elbow and met my eyes. Her expression was pained. "You *are* the best thing that's ever happened to me, Caleb. You're also the worst. I'm trying to reconcile those two things. Help me?"

"How am I supposed to help you?" I asked.

"Tell me your side of things. I want to hear the good and the bad. I have so many questions, so many moments in my life where I only know half the information. You read my side of it. I want your side. Help me understand how I managed to..." Her eyes finished her sentence: *fall in love with you.* "Help me explain it to the rest of the world."

Her words left me reeling. I didn't want the world to know. *I* didn't want to know. In fact, I'd been doing everything within my power to make us both forget where we started. How was this supposed to help?

"It's not for the rest of the world to know, Livvie. I don't understand."

"You wouldn't, but I do. I wouldn't betray your trust. I'd tell it the way it's meant to be told. I'd make them see that some stories aren't black and white. I'd make them feel *this, us.* And then I'd feel better. I wouldn't feel like you got one over on me. I'd feel right about everything between us and I'd defend it. I'll always defend it."

What justification did I have against that? I had what I wanted: assurance that Livvie had no desire to leave me. I'd even managed to sidestep the argument over having broken into her laptop. Most importantly, she'd given me a glimpse of the love she'd once professed to have for me. I was determined to nurture that emotion.

"What do you want to know? For example?" I edged. She leaned toward me and placed a soft kiss on my mouth.

"I hate seeing you like this. If anyone is going to fuck up your face, it should be me." She smiled.

"Think you could take me?" I worked hard not to grin so I wouldn't split my lip open again.

"I think you'd let me."

"Well, you've got me there. I don't think anyone has ever slapped me so many times and walked away without having to look over their shoulder forever." I let my fingers caress her face. I'd slapped her once. "I felt horrible... that one time. I'll never—"

"I know," she interrupted. "I'm sorry I asked about the... you know. I know you're trying to be different and you've changed so much. That wasn't fair."

"You had a right to ask. I'm trying to change, but it doesn't mean I don't struggle with who I used to be. I've had blood on my hands." I silently reflected on my year away from Livvie.

"You're different now," Livvie said softly.

I saw the faces of the women I'd once enslaved and then set free. I thought about the ones I'd been too late to save. They would haunt me forever and it was scarcely penance enough. Yet, fate had brought me to Livvie .

"I don't know that I'm all that different. I'll never stop looking over my shoulder—or yours. I think part of me will always be someone's loyal disciple. It's who I am." I stroked Livvie's hair. "I'd kill for you, Livvie. I'd die for you."

"Caleb. Don't. You're no one's disciple. You're free, and all that shit is behind you." Her arm squeezed my waist.

"I hope you're right, Kitten, but I'd still do anything to protect what's important to me. I just hope it never comes to violence again. From now on, it's just fighting in the gym."

Livvie laughed.

"You mean you did this on purpose? Oh, Caleb," she sighed, "you're such a fucking man sometimes." She kissed me again.

"I'm always a man. Don't you forget it." I winked. "Ask your questions, Kitten. I can't promise I'll always be this agreeable." I skimmed her lower back with my fingers.

Livvie's smile faded a bit, but I could sense her determination nonetheless.

"Why me, Caleb? Why'd you choose *me*?"

I was sorry I invited her questions. I could think of at least ten other things I would rather suffer than formulate words to loaded questions like those. However, *why* is always important to people. It had been important to me. I'd wanted to know why I'd been taken. I'd wanted to know why Rafiq showed me genuine affection when I was a boy. My entire life had been about *why*. I owed Livvie answers.

I cleared my throat.

"You made me curious." I could practically feel the intensity of Livvie's stare. "I watched you for weeks before I decided. Every time I saw you... I wanted to know more about you."

"But why?" She pressed into my side. I let out a huff of air.

"Fuck, I don't know. I guess... you looked kind of sad." I raised my free hand and traced her confused brow. "You liked to stare at the ground and it used to make me angry because I couldn't see your face, your eyes. I wanted to know why you were sad." Listening to my words aloud and staring into those same eyes, I wondered what the hell had ever possessed me to hurt someone so innocent, so beautiful.

"You told me about your mom, about how she treated you, but I didn't know that in the beginning. I saw you in your baggy pants and oversized sweaters and it didn't make any sense to me why such a beautiful girl would hide." I knew she had been hiding from someone like me. I thought, *life is cruel.*

"And then I fucking met you. You ran right into my arms and I..." I almost couldn't say it. "I had to have you. I'm sorry, Livvie. I'm so very sorry."

Livvie shook her head.

"I don't need you to apologize anymore. We're together and I don't need you feeling bad about it. I just want you to stop pushing me." She gripped my shoulder and shook me playfully. "I need to know how we arrived here, but it doesn't mean I'm not happy to be where I am. I'm here, with you. That's nothing either of us should be sorry about."

"It doesn't seem that way sometimes. You care about me, Livvie. I know you do. Except you won't say it because you're punishing me for what I did. I know I deserve it, but stop pretending you've forgiven me. If you want the truth from me, start being honest." I felt the shift in power between us. Livvie had me where she wanted me, but I had her too. We had each other, and I liked knowing it wasn't something either of us could surrender easily.

She put her head down on my chest in supplication. She could ply me so easily sometimes. If I had anything to do with her ability to wield power through submission, then I'd done my best work in Livvie. However, I doubted that was the case. She'd been playing me since the day we met in one fashion or another.

"I forgive you, Caleb. I'm just... angry. You're angry too. I don't like how easily you can hurt me."

"It's not easy, Livvie. I don't *like* hurting you. That's not fair."

She made a growling sound. I almost laughed but managed to hold it in.

"I didn't mean it like that," she said. "I mean... you left. You could leave again. You *think* about leaving and going back to that life. How is that supposed to make me feel?"

I wanted to get up and throw things around the room. Livvie could be so infuriating.

"The only reason I said that is because you do the same to me. One minute you can't live without me and you want me to treat you rough. The next minute you ask me if I've killed someone. Casually! As if I *ever* killed anyone on a whim. Am I supposed to believe you want to spend the rest of your life with someone you think is capable of those things? If so... you're *definitely* not the person I remember."

Livvie smiled.

"The rest of my life? You're ambitious."

I took in a breath and let it out in rush. Yes, she was infuriating. I had to laugh to keep from shaking her.

"I... fine. I'm ambitious." Unable to resist, I added, "It's not like I have anything else to do with forever. My schedule is wide open."

"In that case, can I ask my questions?" She smiled sheepishly.

I sighed.

"Shit. Come on, then."

We spoke for hours, it seemed. How many people had I killed? Why had I killed them? Did I get rid of everyone at the mansion? What happened to Celia (she's very much alive)?

I answered all her questions as quickly and efficiently as I could and without becoming emotional about them. I didn't regret the lives I'd taken. I had never killed indiscriminately. I only felt guilt for those I'd put in harm's way.

I didn't care for the questions involving Rafiq, of which there were few, or the ones having to do with Livvie's and my history, of which there were *many*.

"Did you like the things you did to me?" she asked. I was mentally and physically exhausted.

"Did you?" I asked. I hoped she'd get the hint and stop asking me so many damn questions.

"Some of them," she whispered softly.

I turned my head toward her and stared. She was blushing. Things were finally getting interesting.

"Such as? And don't say the spanking—I *know* you love the spanking."

"I... well, it's *mostly* the spanking, but I like... other stuff too. It's your fault. You've turned me into a sexual deviant like you." She kissed my chest.

I laughed.

"Lucky me."

"You could... tie me up. If you wanted. If you... like that." Livvie's finger slid beneath the sheets and caressed my dick. I groaned.

"Kitten... I'm..." I was distracted. Her fingers wrapped around my flesh and began stroking. "I'm beat all to hell. I don't think..." I trailed off as my eyes slid shut.

"Would you like that, though?" Her voice was small and shy despite the boldness of her touch.

"Yes," I whispered. "I'd like that very much. I miss... god, that feels good." She'd slid her hand to my balls, her nails dragged slightly over the sensitive skin.

"What do you miss?" she whispered. Her leg wound around mine. My hand rested on the small of her back and I could feel her starting to rock against me.

"Control," I managed. "I miss having control." I lifted my hand from her lower back and put it on the back of her head.

"Over me?" she panted.

"Yes. I... liked being able to tell you what to do. I liked knowing what was going to happen next." I laughed to myself. "I liked..." *Breaking you down and making you do*

151

whatever the fuck I wanted you to do. I liked owning you. I liked shocking you. I liked making you come apart and putting you back together. "Stop, Livvie." I placed my hand on hers and kept her from stroking my dick.

"What's wrong?" she asked urgently.

"This!" I sat up slowly. "What do you *think* I liked about it, Livvie? I'm not used to being... I'm not normal, Livvie. I used to get a hard-on when you cried. Is that what you want to hear?"

Livvie's expression was wounded.

"I know that, Caleb. You told me. I don't expect you to be normal. It's just that..." She'd gone from wounded to embarrassed.

"It's what, Livvie? Explain it to me, because you've got me all confused." I stared at her, willing her to answer.

"It's just," she struggled. "Before you... there wasn't anybody. And then we spent all that time together and we did all those things. Then after, I was alone and you were gone and I tried to maybe... with other guys, but they weren't you... and I couldn't..."

"What?" I insisted. "I thought you said you weren't with anybody since me."

She snapped out of her rambling.

"I wasn't! I couldn't! Caleb, the things you *did* to me. I got used to them. I liked them. I could never do anything wrong with you. You told me what to do and... I liked it. There was nobody that could..." She blushed until even her chest looked red.

I exhaled, shocked. I thought about the first morning in the hotel room and the various other times she'd goaded me into dominating her. I felt stupid for not putting it together before. I knew some people enjoyed games involving domination and submission, it's just that it had never been a *game* for me before. I looked at Livvie and smiled.

"Oh, Kitten. What a strange pair we are. I'm... a little speechless. You know what I like. I don't just *like* dominating you—I *love it*. But it's difficult to turn it on and off. It's... different."

Livvie tugged at the sheet between us nervously.

"I know. But... couldn't we try? We've sort of been doing it. Like... just when we're having sex. Couldn't it be like that?"

My brain felt like it was expanding in my skull. She was offering me control, but only under certain circumstances. It was a big concept for me to grasp, but one I was eager to thoroughly comprehend. My dick was fully erect just trying to understand it.

"So if I were to say to you, 'Get down on your knees.' You would say?"

Livvie let out a deep breath and smiled. She slid off the bed and onto the floor.

"Yes, Caleb," she whispered and blushed.

My heart leapt.

"I think... I'm going to like this. *A lot.*"

CHAPTER TWELVE

February. Things were changing. Again. Some of the changes, perhaps even most of them, I enjoyed.

My favorite development had to do with Livvie's thirst to be dominated. Since "The Laptop Incident" and our subsequent pact to be more forthcoming with one another, Livvie had no choice but to break her silence on the subject.

Some of it hadn't been surprising. The sex we'd been having had been undoubtedly familiar to me. I knew Livvie enjoyed being spanked, chased, held down, and occasionally fucked in her ass. What I hadn't anticipated was her desire for what she called *games* and I referred to as *reenactments*.

It had been my hope that upon finding Livvie again, we would start fresh and pretend the past had never occurred (it sounds asinine when I read it back). However, all freshmen are required to take psychology and Livvie seemed to take to it like a duck to water. She wanted to experiment with Exposure Therapy in the hopes that by reliving some of her experiences in a safe environment, she would no longer fear them.

Needless to say, I thought it was a bat-shit crazy idea (that's the technical term). The last thing I wanted was to reprise my role as Livvie's captor. What if it didn't work and she ended up hating me? It took a great deal of convincing from Livvie, but ultimately I'd agreed to some of the less... disturbing moments.

One morning I made us breakfast, put it on a wheeled cart from IKEA, and took it into Livvie's room. Livvie had taken the time to prepare herself while I cooked breakfast, and I'd been pleasantly surprised to find her wearing one of my white button-up shirts and a dainty pair of kitten ears. I understood the significance of the shirt. The ears were a nice touch. I felt that touch center mass.

"Should I take my shirt off?" I asked. History dictated I should.

"If you're over your *self-indulgent modesty*," she whispered. In the past, I would have found her words incendiary—another time, another place—but in our reimagining I found them to be... charming.

I'd removed my shirt, enjoying the way Livvie's eyes lusted instead of feared. I took a chance and played along.

"It's a pity I have nothing to bind you with. I'd be hard-pressed to recall anyone who looks as good as you do in a collar and shackles."

Livvie turned and brought me a box from beneath her bed. Inside I found a jeweled collar, a leash, and a pair of fuzzy handcuffs. I laughed.

"Oh my, you have been a busy girl. When and where did you get these?"

Livvie blushed and the memory was further reshaped.

"I ordered them online," she said timidly. Her hands were already behind her back and she swayed gently from side to side.

I kissed her. It was a light meeting of lips, a token.

"Turn around," I ordered. Livvie shivered and a small sound escaped her lips. She complied quickly.

As I fed Livvie breakfast while she knelt at my feet, I was struck by several thoughts. First, I realized the power of forgiveness. Second, I found Livvie's game enticing. Third, I could never leave Livvie. Fourth, I never *wanted* to leave her.

For better or worse, Livvie had been irrevocably altered by her experiences with me. She was a nineteen-year-old with proclivities no one her age would understand and a vulnerability any creep like me could easily spot and take advantage of. She was strong, smart, willful, and driven, but she was also soft, trusting, and needy where her heart was concerned. Livvie needed taking care of.

Other changes in our relationship I didn't enjoy quite as much. As part of our pact, Livvie and I discussed our fears, hopes, and aspirations for what our relationship could be. She wanted to know more about my past, Mexico, and the less gruesome ways I'd spent my year away from her.

Also, I wasn't comfortable with Livvie's writing. However, aside from the time we spent with Claudia and Rubio—or having sex—there seemed little else occupying Livvie's and my time. Apparently, I'd inspired her to go "back to the drawing board." She wanted to incorporate more of the facts I'd given her.

Suddenly, there were days when she wouldn't speak to me because she'd just finished rehashing some traumatic event involving me. There were some moments neither of us wanted to *re-imagine*. At first I tried try to seduce her away from her thoughts, but after the first few times she began to see it as manipulative. Soon after, I decided to make myself scarce during her periods of... well, her periods.

Other days, she took to cornering me on the sofa or at the dinner table to ask me invasive questions about my past. These usually ended in an argument over my "evasiveness" or sex. Sometimes we had both—an argument first, and sex right after. I worried that if it kept up, I'd get an erection every time she looked upset with me.

Yet, as with our sexual games, I began to see the merit in expressing myself through my conversations with Livvie. I began to realize I wasn't as upset by her questioning as I had been before. In slow gradations, I found myself offering information she hadn't asked about. I told her about RezA and how guilty I had felt for not warning him Narweh was dead. He'd been such an optimistic person. He hadn't enjoyed his slavery any more than I had, but where I'd been rebellious unto my own ruination, RezA had navigated his situation with grace.

"Do you think he could have escaped? I mean, I've heard that gun go off. The whole neighborhood probably knew someone had been shot. Couldn't he have heard it and escaped?" Livvie asked.

This is going to sound absolutely ridiculous but... it hadn't fucking occurred to me! It really hadn't. I'd been out of my mind. To this day, whenever I recall the moment of my first kill, there is no sound beyond the beating of my heart and the high-pitched wail of adrenaline in my veins. I remember the heavy weight of the gun. I remember the look of disgust on Narweh's face. I remember shutting my eyes and squeezing the trigger. I remember something wet splattering on my face before I hit the ground. I remember the silence.

I sat up and I heard nothing. I stared into Narweh's cold, empty eyes. I remember thinking the soul must be real. Something had been keeping Narweh alive. That something was gone. There was only meat, blood, and bones left behind.

I remember an acute feeling of anger and sorrow that I had not been brave enough to keep my eyes open. I remember thinking: *I should have made him beg for my forgiveness. I should have made him plead for mercy. I should have raped him with the cane he used to beat me.*

"I... don't know if RezA could have escaped. I suppose it's possible," I said. I was dumbfounded. "Rafiq said he burned the building down with Narweh inside it. I guess... I didn't want to ask too many questions."

"Why?" Livvie's hand rested on top of mine.

"I wasn't sure Rafiq would like it," I said simply. "I figured if he could burn a building full of people down and chat about it over breakfast, I had no business getting on his bad side."

"How old were you?"

"I'd have to do the math. When's my birthday?"

"James. Seriously?"

I laughed.

"Give me a break. I've never had to remember before."

"You're twenty-seven." She smiled a little sadly. I let myself think for a moment.

"I guess I was... twelve, maybe thirteen?"

Livvie sat back in her chair and stared at me.

"Jesus." She shook her head and wiped at her eye.

"I'm fine, Pet. At least... I think?" I didn't mind opening up to Livvie (much), but afterward there was always the worry she would see me as weak. I didn't want her pity. I only wanted her to understand why it took so much effort on my part to give her what she needed. Though I was beginning to learn that what I thought Livvie needed and what she actually needed were sometimes two different things. Not often, but sometimes. There were days I could take my job as Livvie's protector overboard (drunk college boys should watch their mouths if they value having teeth).

"You're better than fine. I'm so damn impressed with you. I feel like... the more I learn about your past... I had all these feelings I couldn't process in Mexico. When I tried to explain them to Reed or Sloan, I could see on their faces how ridiculous they thought I was."

"It's easier to explain your feelings for an abused whore than a man who held you prisoner. Is that about the size and shape of it?" I kept the sound of my balls shriveling from my voice.

Livvie appeared horrified.

"No! James... no. It's more like... you could be so cold. But when I was at my lowest, when I felt like I was hanging on by a thread... you always knew what to say. You have this ability to hold me and make me believe you. You're full of warmth and kindness."

I had to scoff at that, and Livvie slapped my arm.

"You *are!*" she insisted. "I couldn't even see you in that room sometimes, but I could still feel it. I didn't understand where it came from, but when I hear you talk about the past it all makes sense to me."

Admittedly, I was a little embarrassed. I'm not really accustomed to compliments, especially when they're intensely personal and genuine. The void almost felt... full. I, on the other hand, felt squirmy.

"Well then. Good. I suppose. It's good that you think I'm... nice."

"James, you look like I just farted in your general direction." She grinned.

"What! That's disgusting."

Livvie laughed. It was her incredibly loud cackle that meant she couldn't control herself. It was not a pretty sight, but I loved it when she laughed like that. I *love* it when she laughs like that.

"No. It's *Monty Python.*"

I was laughing too. Livvie's laughter is too infectious not to take part in it.

"A what?"

"It's a movie." She wiped tears from her eyes.

I pulled her hand toward my mouth and licked her finger. There are so many kinds of tears. I plan to collect them all.

"I'm not sure I want to see it."

Livvie leaned forward and kissed my lips.

"Well, we *have* to now. It's an older movie and over-the-top ridiculous, but I can't wait to see your face."

I made a face of the "what the hell is wrong with you?" variety.

"It's disturbing when you do that. I always know when something big is about to happen because there you are, staring at me with your huge doe eyes."

Livvie shrugged.

"Not my fault you're so nice to look at." Her expression turned ruefully judgmental. "You're the only person I know who looks *sexier* with bruises." She poked the butterfly stitch on my eyebrow and I hissed.

"Dammit, Pet. That hurts." I'd been visiting the gym a few times a week and sparring. I fought Fernando mostly, but other fighters from time to time. Some of them were even decent conversationalists, so long as the topic didn't stray from matches, fighting styles, or food intake. I was compelled to try a protein shake... once.

"Oh? And it didn't hurt when that guy kicked you in the face?" She made a fist and twisted it near the corner of her eye while sticking out her bottom lip.

"Are you calling me a cry baby?" I stood and glared. Livvie's head was craned all the way back to meet my eyes. "Big talk for such a little girl."

"I'm not scared of you. I'll poke your band-aid." She puffed out her ample chest.

It was difficult to keep a straight face. Had I really been outmatched by *her*? The answer was a resounding *yes*.

"You poke my band-aid and you're going to have a serious problem."

She sucked in her cheeks to keep from smiling. Slowly her hand reached up toward my eyebrow. Her eyes met mine. She considered. A flicker of excitement caused her to lick her bottom lip. She pressed her fingertip to my cut. I didn't wince.

"Is this the part where I get angry and threaten to teach you a lesson?" I asked calmly. Livvie practically vibrated with excitement.

"Yes." She shivered.

"When do you leave for work?"

"I have a few hours." She sounded breathy.

"Well then." I caressed her face so I could watch the way she closed her eyes to savor my touch. With my other hand, I grabbed a fistful of hair and pulled. "Let's go teach you some manners."

***

"Remind me again. Why are we spending our romantic evening with Claudia and Rubio? If romance is what you're after, it seems counterproductive to have other people in attendance." I'd forgotten my shoes in my hotel room and we were forced to go and retrieve them. The clock in my dash display reminded me we were supposed to pick up the other couple in an hour.

"*Because*, Best Boyfriend in the World, it'll be fun. Also, Rubi really wanted to take Claudia somewhere nice. He's been saving up since Christmas. Can Fabes is supposed to have amazing food. I still don't know how you managed to make reservations. How *did* you get reservations anyway? It was pretty short notice." Livvie checked her lipstick in the visor mirror for the third time. I think she just liked the way her lips looked in red. So did I.

"It was short notice because you didn't tell me I was supposed to plan something. Valentine's Day? I've heard of it, but I had no idea people actually participated in such... sentimentality. Don't they get enough of that during Thanksgiving and Christmas?" I put my blinker on and moved to the passing lane to get around someone in what appeared to be a golf cart. *Fuel-efficient cars. Bleh!*

"Changing the subject, James. I'm on to your tactics." Livvie glared. A smile played on her lips.

"I went down to the restaurant in person and charmed the hostess. She was very amenable." I grinned. Livvie's smile turned sour. "You asked." I shrugged.

"I didn't ask you to flirt with another girl."

"I didn't say I flirted. I said I was charming. I simply explained that I was a cad who'd made the grievous mistake of not acquiring reservations to take my beautiful girlfriend and her entourage to dinner on the most romantic day of the year. I told her I'd be lost without you and that anything she could do to help me keep your favor would be worthy of my deepest gratitude. Then I tipped her a day's wages." I kept my eyes forward, though I knew my expression remained smug.

"Asshole," Livvie said. She grabbed my hand and put it in both of hers, squeezing.

"Idiot," I countered. "As if anyone else could hold my attention." I squeezed her hand in return.

"I got you a present," she said.

"Kitten," I admonished. "We already exchanged gifts." I'd given her pearls. She'd gifted me with the sight of her in a red cape and heels high enough to nearly put us at eye level. It had been a very short but enjoyable chase. No one could run in those things. I forbid her to wear them outside the house.

"Relax. It's no big deal." She opened her purse and took out a box of candy. I laughed.

"It looks open."

"I ate most of them," she said.

"You are so strange sometimes, Pet."

"Method to my madness, Sexy. Open your hand." I complied and she put the heart-shaped candies in my palm. When I looked at them, I felt as though someone had squeezed my heart. All the candies read "Be Mine."

"I'm already yours, Pet. And you're mine." Stuffing my mouth full of candy hearts may have lessened the romance of the moment, but Livvie didn't seem to mind.

"Yes, yours," she said. She kissed my cheek.

I felt in my heart the affirmation of what I had come to suspect was true for some time. What she really meant was: *I love you.*

After retrieving my shoes and picking up Claudia and Rubio (I have never been comfortable with calling that man Rubi), we arrived at the restaurant with ten minutes to spare. I felt the slightest bit awkward as we approached the hostess. She was the same woman from the week before and she smiled warmly. However, I didn't miss the way her eyebrow lifted as she saw the young crowd I'd brought with me. I could never be ashamed of Livvie, but traveling with three younger people made me feel... old. There had been a time when it wouldn't have bothered me because I had no idea of my age. Regardless, the hostess greeted us warmly.

"Señor Cole." She pointed us in the direction of our waiter, who greeted us with a smile and asked us to follow him.

"Your last name is Cole? Like Sophia's?" Claudia sounded incredulous.

"Strange coincidence," I said.

Claudia shrugged and it made her look younger, despite the very adult cocktail dress she was wearing.

"I guess if you ever get married you won't argue about whether or not Sophia will change her name."

"Claudia," Livvie hissed.

The waiter averted his gaze with a tight-lipped smile as he ushered us into our seats. I helped Livvie out of her coat and pulled out her chair (six months prior I couldn't open a door). Rubio, upon witnessing my impeccable boyfriend skills, assisted Claudia. The ladies seemed to appreciate it very much.

"I will give you a moment to go over the menu while I check your coats." The waiter walked away with the coats. I watched him speak to the hostess and surmised she was supposed to check our coats when we arrived. I hoped I didn't get her into any trouble. Then again, she should have done her job.

"Thank you for inviting us," Rubio said to me. He is ever the gentleman, and I often wonder how Claudia has managed to keep him. Then I am reminded of me and Livvie. Stranger things have happened.

"Thank you for helping me choose the restaurant. I'm not overly familiar with the area." I winked and Rubio repressed a smile. The concierge at my hotel had told me about the restaurant, but there was no·harm in helping Rubio impress his date.

"Rubi is so modest." Claudia turned to her boyfriend. "You never told me you helped plan this." She kissed him on the cheek. Rubio blushed (poor bastard).

"It was… a surprise."

Livvie's hand squeezed my thigh.

"Aww, you guys are so sweet you're going to make me puke." She and I laughed at the other couple's discomfort. Did they have any idea whom they were out to dinner with?

Claudia composed herself quickly.

"Like you guys are any better. You're always undressing each other with your eyes. I'm surprised you even left the house."

"A man has to eat," I said. "Also, I undress her with more than my eyes. Sometimes I use my teeth." Livvie blushed to her roots while the rest of us laughed.

"I'm just glad she finally met someone. Rubi and I were trying to set her up for a while. We thought she might be gay and ashamed to tell us. I even told her about kissing my friend Bettany so she would come out, but she never did." Claudia has a tendency to impart too much information, but when it comes to Livvie, I often enjoy what she has to say.

"You don't *have* a friend named Bettany," Livvie said. She sounded put-out, but it was all for show.

"You didn't know that," said Claudia. "I was just trying to let you know I was okay with you being gay."

"But I'm not gay!" Livvie said with mock exasperation. She covered her face when the waiter chose that exact moment to return to our table.

Though I was sure he had overheard, the waiter kept a professional demeanor. We all managed to compose ourselves enough to order dinner and wine. Livvie thought Europe was "awesome" for no other reason than a person could drink legally drink at age eighteen. Of course, if you could reach the bar they'd serve you.

"You know, if you ever want to experiment with a woman—under my close guidance, of course—I'd be alright with it." I smiled cheekily toward Livvie and lifted a brow for good measure.

Livvie shook her head.

"I bet you would." Her hand cupped my balls beneath the table. Her eyes widened as she felt the stirring of my arousal. "Later," she whispered. I wondered if she meant she'd please me later, or if I'd get to see her kiss and touch another woman later. Either way—lucky me.

The rest of dinner went on in the same jovial fashion. Claudia and Livvie took care of most of the conversation. I preferred it that way, and Rubio seemed to as well. Livvie was witty and Claudia so uncouth that one couldn't help but be amused by the pair of them. The sprite and her boyfriend were growing on me—like a fungus.

After dinner and an attempt at dancing (I am *not* a good dancer), I returned Claudia and Rubio home. Rubio, being the gentleman that he is, tried to slip his share of dinner into my pocket, but I wouldn't allow it.

"Buy her something expensive. Nothing makes a woman more agreeable in the bedroom," I said with a grin.

"I'm already agreeable," retorted Claudia. "Rubi may seem quiet, but you know what they say about the quiet ones."

Rubi laughed even as he blushed.

"She's drunk. I better take her inside."

"Yes! Take me!" Claudia pulled Rubio toward her and mauled his face with her mouth. It went on so long I decided to drive off. I saw Rubio wave as he kept kissing.

Livvie was stretched out in the passenger seat. She was blissfully drunk, and by the way she was rubbing herself, I knew I'd have my own hands full once we got home.

"Is there anything you need from your apartment? I'd rather stay at the hotel tonight." I stroked her with one hand whenever I wasn't shifting.

"Why?" she asked dreamily.

"All of my things are in my hotel room. Your apartment is closer to where we are. We may as well stop and get your things if you need something," I said. I hated sleeping without Livvie. The nightmares were significantly diminished when she was next to me.

"But I want you. I don't want to wait," she whined. She was very intoxicated, and part of me suspected there would be no sex for me that night.

"I want you, too. It's a pity we live so far apart. Claudia and Rubio don't have that problem."

Livvie suddenly seemed very sober, if you didn't take her huge eyes into consideration.

"Are you... do you want to move into my apartment?"

"No," I said definitively.

"Oh." She seemed at once relieved and disappointed. She turned away and stared out the window for a few minutes, then, angrily, "Why not?"

"Because your apartment is small."

"Oh." Confusion.

I sighed.

"I'm asking you to move in with me, Sophia. I'll leave the hotel, you'll leave your apartment, and we'll buy a place that's *ours*." Silence filled the vehicle for what felt like endless hours.

"Okay," she said simply.

"Okay?" I asked, incredulous. What sort of response was that?

"Okay," she repeated and put her hand in mine.

"Okay," I said.

The void was overflowing.

CHAPTER THIRTEEN

We moved into our new flat in April. Though I thought otherwise, Livvie insisted it was the perfect birthday gift to move into our new home on her birthday. She'd insisted her birthday was just the leverage she would need to coerce her friends into helping her move her things. She didn't want movers, she said. It made her feel awkward enough that I had purchased our home and put it in her name. I insisted it was better than putting it in the name of someone who didn't legally exist. She agreed but couldn't abide by making strangers move her.

For my part, I was something akin to excited. It seems wrong for a man to be "excited"; it sounds too much like an emotion for a school girl. I'd wanted to buy the house outright, but I thought that might be suspicious if the FBI decided to poke around. Instead, I had Livvie remove the amount of the down payment from her fund and put it in a safe deposit box. I then used that sum of cash to pay the bank.

Eventually, I was going to have to enlist the help of some former acquaintances to keep up appearances where Livvie's new lifestyle was concerned. The FBI couldn't necessarily touch us in Spain, but it was best not to provoke attention by living outside the means they knew Livvie was capable of. For better or worse, I didn't tell Livvie about my plans involving illicit activity. I was becoming a very well-behaved boyfriend, but I was still me.

We'd purchased an enormous property that had been vacant for some time. Livvie and I had a good laugh over the number of windows. There was hardly a dark corner to be found, and light flooded every nook and cranny. I thought it very apropos. We'd spent enough time in the dark. However, because there were *some* things I liked to do with Livvie that should never see the light of day, I made sure the bedrooms had drapes.

The home had been furnished to best display its vaulted ceilings, marble countertops, bowl sinks, sunken living rooms, and wood and stone accoutrements. I'd made an offer to purchase it as it was. It was the perfect excuse to talk Livvie into donating her furniture to Claudia and Rubio (let *him* deal with all the bed pillows). She's raised her eyebrows at me, but ultimately didn't resist. I'd already been looking at houses for some time. By the time Livvie and I started taking tours, I'd narrowed the list significantly. It had been a test of my cunning to push Livvie toward "choosing" the flat I wanted on her own. I was ultimately successful.

All in all, the home suggested a certain level of wealth, but not enough to raise eyebrows. Our neighbors were professionals, not celebrities. It was the sort of place we could grow into and live in for quite some time. I planned on converting one of the larger rooms upstairs into a library/office for Livvie. I'd already claimed the downstairs for a project of my later choosing.

"*Please* tell me this is the last box." Claudia lay sprawled on the hardwood floor.

"I don't have that much stuff, Claudia. Stop whining." Livvie put down the box she was carrying and wiped sweat from her forehead with the back of her hand. I caught her looking around with a wondrous expression and my chest expanded. Making her happy was more reward than I'd ever expected. I was once again struck by a sense of purpose. One I could take pride in.

I stepped over Claudia and spoke to Livvie. "There's Coke in the fridge. I picked some up, along with a case of water. I'll go to the grocery in a little while for more supplies. I owe you a birthday dinner at the very least." I kissed Livvie on the forehead on my way out the door. The moving van was empty and Rubio was going to follow me to drop it off and bring me back.

He was waiting for me outside. He was actually dressed for function instead of fashion. It was amusing to see him in loose jeans, sneakers, and a t-shirt. He looked even younger than he already was.

"Are you ready to go?" he asked.

"Yes. The women can handle the unpacking while we're gone. I want to stop at the grocery on the way back. We can pick up some steaks for dinner." I ruffled Rubio's hair as I passed him. He laughed and turned toward his car. I'd never done more than shake his hand until that moment. However, over the last few months we'd become friends of a kind. I could never confide in him, but he looked up to me and I'd begun to take him under my wing, so to speak.

"Sounds good. We can pick up a cake for Sophia." He smiled. He'd sort of taken me under his wing as well. Rubio gave me insight into Livvie's youth. She was downplaying the importance of her birthday, but he knew she still wanted a little spectacle. I planned on giving her quite the spectacle later when we were alone. But cake was nice too.

"Great idea," I said. As I pulled away, I couldn't help but look at Livvie's and my new home in the rearview. Had I really moved on? Had I left the man I was behind? I didn't know for certain. However, the knowledge that Livvie would be the first person I saw every morning and the last person I would see every night was more comfort than I'd ever allowed myself. My new life with her was everything. As much as it terrified me to think I was nothing without her, I was only too happy to have her for any amount of time fate would allow. Of course, if and when fate decided to try and wrest her from my arms, I would fight like the bastard I was to keep her.

After we dropped off the van, Rubio and I picked up some groceries and a cake for Livvie. I was exhausted, but I was looking forward to making Livvie's birthday special. Selfishly, I couldn't wait until everyone else left and Livvie and I could enjoy our first night in our new home.

"I hope Sophia likes our gift. We're not ballin' out of control like you." Rubio grinned and tossed some of his fastidious hair out of his face. I was constantly tempted to take scissors to it.

"I'm sure she'll love whatever it is. You're her friends—you probably know her better than I do."

"I don't think so. She's different with you. She's happier. When Claudia and I first met her, she was kinda quiet. She didn't like to talk about things: her family, where she grew up. Claudia felt sorry for her, said she must be very lonely."

I frowned.

"Sophia doesn't need anyone's pity. She's too strong for that."

"Not like that." Rubio appeared wounded. "Claudia just doesn't like to see people unhappy. She doesn't show it, but she's very sensitive. She has a very big heart."

"Right," I said, incredulous. The sprite was brash and rude. I liked her, but I had my doubts about her soft mushy insides.

Rubio, for the first time, looked irritated.

"You wouldn't know, would you? *I do.*"

I had to laugh.

"I didn't mean to offend you. Claudia is a good friend. She's just... well, you know."

Rubio's anger faded quickly.

"Yes. I know. The night we met, a friend of mine dragged me to a party. There was a girl I liked and I was heartbroken because I found out she started seeing someone else. I wanted to stay home but I went out anyway. Claudia saw me and she came over to me. She's a big ball of happy energy and she insisted I cheer up. I told her about the girl and she told me to forget about her because I was *her* boyfriend." Rubio had a stupid grin on his face.

"You belong together," I said. Rubio seemed to like that. "Tell me more about Sophia."

"She used to be sad. We cheered her up, but only for so long. I used to leave her and Claudia alone sometimes because I think it upset Sophia to see us so happy. She never said, but it was a vibe we got. That's why we tried to set her up so much." He shrugged. "Then she met you. She's happy now. I hope you understand how lucky you are. I don't know much about her past, but I know she is a good person. You should be careful with her."

I looked at Rubio and his expression was very serious. Rubio was a good man.

"I plan to make Sophia very happy, Rubio. You don't have to tell me what I have."

"Good," he said. "I never want to fight you."

I laughed. I couldn't help it. I was picturing Rubio trying to fight me.

"I never want that either, Rubio."

Things were considerably less pleasant when we finally arrived home. Claudia met us in the driveway and the expression on her face gave me heart palpitations.

"Where is she?" I asked. I was already rushing toward the house. I didn't hear what Claudia was trying to tell me.

"Sophia!" I yelled. I bounded up the stairs.

"I'm in here!" she responded from the bedroom. A wave of relief shivered through me. She was safe. There was no danger. Our lives were different. It took me a moment to settle. I'd thought I was going to have to hurt someone.

When I walked into the bedroom, Livvie was sitting on the bed. She'd been crying, and there was a letter in her hands.

"What's wrong, Pet?"

She shrugged.

"I don't know. I just…" She wiped at her eyes and sniffled.

"What happened? Did I do something?" I hated when Livvie was sad. I no longer relished the sight of those tears. They were bitter on my tongue.

"No, Baby. It's not you." She'd never called me *baby* before—well, not in a positive way.

"Tell me." I sat next to her on the bed and she instantly found her way under my arm and against my chest. I rubbed her back and waited. Livvie was a talker and I knew she'd come out with it eventually.

"My mom sent me a birthday card. I brought my mail over and there was an unmarked envelope. I wasn't ready for it." She buried herself further in my chest.

Livvie's relationship with her family presented a quandary. I wanted her to be happy. I wanted her to have all the things she desired. However, I wanted to be a part of her happiness. I wanted to be the largest part. Her family could threaten that—they could threaten *us*, what we had. I needed to tread carefully.

"What did it say?"

"That she's sorry. She says she misses me, that they all miss me: my brothers, my sisters. She wants to know if we can work things out." Livvie sobbed and held me tighter.

"Is that what you want, Pet?" I wanted her to say no. I wanted her to say I was the only person she needed and to hell with the rest of them. But I knew what that would mean. I'd been orphaned. I might have one living parent, but as far as I was concerned I was *still* an orphan.

"I don't know."

I sighed.

"It's me. It's always me. I don't want to be the thing that keeps you from the people you love." I wasn't sure what I was trying to say, I just knew it hurt like hell to say it. Livvie's relationship with me was always going to alienate her from the rest of the world and I was too selfish to change that.

"You don't!" Livvie insisted. "Things were shit between us before you and I ever met. You *know* that, it's just..."

"She's your mother. They're your blood."

"So are you." She kissed my chest and went back to lying against me. "We've bled for each other. That's more than I can say for my 'blood'."

I inhaled sharply. While I found her words moving, they were also troubling.

"That was my fault too."

"Caleb, is this about you? Are you *trying* to make me angry with you? You make me happy. Today was one of the best days I've ever had. Don't ruin it by making this about us. This is about my mom and the way she manipulates everything. At least you had reasons for what you did to me. She's my mother. What the fuck were *her* reasons, Caleb? What were her reasons for treating me like shit and then waiting *five days* to come see me in the hospital?" Livvie sat up. Her fists were clenched around what I presumed was her birthday card.

175

"I'm sorry, Kitten. I didn't mean to make it about me. Here's what I know: You deserve to be happy. If getting the answers to your questions is going to give you peace, you owe yourself that much. If you're done with her, that's okay too... but I don't think you are." I pulled her back into my arms. I didn't know if I did it to comfort her or myself, but it seemed to help us both.

"Maybe I'll call her next week."

"Okay," I whispered. It was all I could manage.

"Promise me you won't leave." Livvie's arms gripped me tight.

"I promise. Can you say the same?" I almost dreaded the answer.

"I promise. I'm yours," she said.

"And I'm yours."

"Sophia? Should we go?" Claudia shouted from downstairs.

"No!" Livvie said. "We'll be down in a minute." She sat up and kissed me, softly at first, and then passionately. I pulled her to me and caressed her breasts. She broke the kiss. "Later, Sexy. We have all the time in the world."

"I plan to hold you to that." I kissed her one more time.

"Good. I love it when you hold me." She smiled and I could see she was in a better place.

I went downstairs to keep our friends company while Livvie cleaned herself up. Once she came down, we dined on *arroz con gandules* and steak. We had birthday cake for dessert, and I will always remember the smile on Livvie's face when she blew out her candles.

That night, after everyone else had left and we were finally alone, Livvie and I sat on our new sofa and stared into the flames of our new fireplace.

"Thank you, James. I had a great birthday."

I chuckled.

"Moving boxes, emotional trauma, and birthday cake—you're easy to please."

She nudged my ribs.

"Butthead."

"I'll let you have that one since it's your birthday."

"Speaking of, do I get a present?" I could hear the smile in her voice.

"Yes. Do you want it?" I coaxed.

"Of course!"

"Very well, but first… I believe it's customary to give the birthday girl a spanking."

Livvie squirmed.

"But… I'm so tired!"

"Good. Less chance of you moving around so much." I adjusted our bodies and placed her over my lap. It was the most uninspired spanking I've ever delivered. She giggled through the entirety of it and I did nothing to curb her behavior.

"Aww, you went soft on me." She was still laughing between panting breaths.

"There are no drapes in the living room. I don't want to scare the neighbors just yet."

"Oh. My. God. I forgot about the windows." She scrambled up and sat in my lap. "They probably think we're perverts."

"Aren't we?"

"Good point. Now, kind sir, my present please." She held out both hands. I lifted her off my lap and we walked upstairs.

I'm going to interject now and tell you upfront that I won't be sharing the details of my gift to Livvie. Don't pout! It's simply too embarrassing to rehash. However, as I don't want to read the incessant questions about it on the internet, I'll tell you this: It involved recreating another of Livvie's memories… of me… alone… in the shower. Make your own panties wet! I'm moving on to the next chapter.

CHAPTER FOURTEEN

I was dreaming. I hate it when I dream, but for the first time in recent memory... it was good. I was having the kind of dream a person doesn't wish to wake up from. Rafiq was there, but it wasn't really him. It was a version of him I'd never know and that he could never be. His presence made it obvious I was dreaming, but his company added something and I chose to go along.

Livvie and I were having a party. We were celebrating my birthday. There were lots of people I didn't recognize, but Livvie seemed to know them. I think one of them was her mother. They were in the kitchen together, pouring champagne into long flutes. One of Livvie's sisters was trying to convince them she could have a glass. She looked the way I imagine Livvie looked as a child. Livvie looked so happy.

"You've done well, *Khoya*. I'm proud of you. You deserve this," Rafiq said. He clapped me on the back and ruffled my hair the way he used to when I was a boy. I swatted his hand away.

"I'm not a child. Stop doing that." I couldn't stop smiling.

"I know. You're a man now. You have a family of your own. Perhaps I am only reminiscing over the boy I knew." He ruffled my hair again and I didn't mind.

"I'm glad you could come. I don't have any other family."

"We're orphans, Caleb. We make our own families." I laughed.

"Yes, I remember."

"And the rest? Do you remember that as well?" Sadness had crept into his voice.

"I forgave you. It's all led me here." I looked toward Livvie and her mother. They waved at me and I raised a hand to acknowledge them.

"Who's this guy? He looks rather interesting and scary." Claudia bumped into my side and nearly pushed me into Rafiq.

"Do you always have to be so forceful?"

"I don't like it when I'm not the center of attention." She winked.

"It's *my* birthday!" I chided. Claudia shrugged.

I introduced Claudia to Rafiq and made a hasty exit. She was already asking him intimate questions about his role in my life. Rafiq looked like he'd smelled something foul and I laughed. He deserved it.

As I walked into the main living room, Rubio was working on connecting the PlayStation. He turned toward me when I came in.

"Give me a hand, James? I can't seem to do anything in these ridiculously skinny pants." Rubio is a quiet guy. My head couldn't create inventive dialogue for him.

I couldn't quite put the PlayStation together either.

"I'm dreaming, Rubio. I can't put this shit together. Hold on." I kicked the PlayStation and all the cables were magically connected.

"Nice! Someday, when Claudia stops coddling me like an infant, I hope you can teach me how to be more of a man," Rubio said (it's my dream—stop judging me).

"You can start by taking care of this." I took out a pair of scissors from my pocket and cut the large hank of hair covering most of his face. There was a large round of applause.

"Okay everyone, it's time to sing *Happy Birthday!*" The crowd parted for Livvie as she walked out of the kitchen holding a large chocolate cake covered in candles.

Happy birthday to you.
Happy birthday to you.
Happy birthday dear, James.
Happy birthday to you.

I scrunched my face. When had I learned that song?
Wake up, Birthday Boy. It's time for one of your presents.

Something soft touched my face.
Wake up, Sexy. It's your birthday.

I smiled both inside and outside the dream. *Livvie.*
She was real. She was with me. She was mine. If the
dream had been good—and it had been—waking up had
been even better.

I opened my eyes slowly. Reality and fantasy rearranged themselves in my mind until everything was clear.
I smiled when I saw Livvie standing by the side of the
bed. She raised her arm and tickled my face with a long
feather. I rubbed my nose.

"That's not what that's for," I said. My voice was
rough. I yawned and stretched.

"Want me to tickle your penis?" She flicked the
feather over the tent in the sheets.

I put my hand over my erection and turned away.

"No. That's not for you. I have to go to the bathroom."

"Well get up! I have a whole day of birthday activities
planned and you're spoiling my fun with your sleeping...
and your pee boner."

I laughed.

"I hate when you call it that."

"Yeah? Well I hate that I can't play with it. Why the
hell is it so hard if I'm not supposed to play with it?
That's false advertising, Mister."

I flopped onto my back and threw my arms across
my eyes.

"Fine. Ravage me. But don't expect to go anywhere for a while." The last time she mounted my morning erection I couldn't come for over an hour. Livvie had to take a nap when we finished and the whole morning had been appropriated.

"Le sigh. It's going to have to wait. We have plans. Now, *get up!*" Livvie put her hands on my stomach and bounced me up and down.

"Stop!" I *really* had to piss. I grabbed Livvie around her waist and pulled her into the bed with me. She squealed as I tickled her. "I'm going to do this until you pee!" Her legs were kicking, but I threw the comforter over them until she was trapped.

"Oh, god! Oh, please. Please stop!" She was laughing despite the panic I could see in her eyes.

"Are you sorry?" I teased.

"Yes! Please!" Livvie was panting by the time I stopped tickling her. She smiled up at me.

"Can I kiss you?" I asked.

"You haven't brushed your teeth." She wrinkled her nose.

"I know. That's why I asked." I was already leaning down toward her mouth. I kept it brief. I hopped off of her quickly and made my way into the bathroom before she could try to retaliate.

There was a knock on the door.

"Meet me downstairs when you're done. I made breakfast."

"Okay," I said.

Once I was done using the bathroom, I washed my hands and brushed my teeth. As I wiped my face on a purple hand towel (Livvie had worked her frilly girl-magic in our bathroom), I stared at myself in the mirror. It was

my first birthday. I was twenty-eight. The feeling was surreal. I wondered if I looked my age.

*This is my life. I was a whore in my youth, a killer since my
adolescence, and a monster as a man. Who am I now? What am I
now?* I shrugged.

Livvie and I had been living together for about four
months. It had taken some getting used to in the beginning. I wasn't accustomed to having another person
around me every day. Although, having already spent so
much time with Livvie during her captivity and also having made every effort to see her often while we were
dating made it somewhat easier to adjust. If I needed to
hide out for a while, I would usually go upstairs to work
on Livvie's library/office some more. Otherwise, I was
downstairs working on building new sets to exorcise my
perversions (a few of the perversions were *her* ideas). Livvie made me put a lock on the door so no one would
accidentally stumble across it.

Livvie didn't seem to have much of an adjusting issue
at all. She explained she was used to a house full of loud
people. If anything, she sometimes didn't like the size of
the house. She said it was so big it felt empty sometimes.
However, Claudia and Rubio practically lived with us, so
that didn't last very long. On the days Livvie needed to be
alone, she was usually upstairs writing on her laptop.

I was ever changing and discovered that while some
things would always make me uncomfortable—Livvie's
new phone-relationship with her mother, meeting new
people, attending film festivals (I love Livvie, but some of
those people are so dull!), and explaining my lack of actual
employment—I was happy being James. Admittedly,
there were moments when I missed my former life, but
for the most part I was becoming more comfortable with

my new life and the things that came with it: Livvie, friends, and… birthdays.

Livvie was impatiently waiting for me once I reached the bottom of the stairs. She'd made small pancakes with strawberries and bacon. They were arranged in a smile on my plate.

"I was expecting a bowl of cereal," I quipped.

"Don't worry, I'm saving that for tomorrow," she replied. She came around the counter and put her hands on my face. "Happy birthday, Sexy." She pressed her lips to mine. She tasted like orange juice and syrup. I chased the sweetness of her tongue, pulling her toward me until I felt her go soft in my arms.

Livvie once told me I stole her breath when we kissed. She said it was as though I filtered the very air she breathed into her lungs. I thought it was more of her flowery words. However, once the thought was planted in my mind, I began to pay particular attention. Yes, I felt something too. I loved the moment Livvie gave herself to me. She became nothing but her instincts. She swayed. She whimpered. She rubbed against me.

I let my hands travel down her back and over her rounded ass. I pulled up her skirt. I was seconds away from putting my thumbs in her panties and pulling them down when my efforts were thwarted.

"No, Sexy, not right now." She put her hands behind her in an attempt stop my mauling.

"Yes," I said. "Right now." I grabbed her hands and held them in my left. With my free hand I began slipping her panties down. I placed sucking kisses across her shoulder.

"James," she groaned. "The windows."

I sighed.

"Dammit! I'm putting in drapes. Today!" I said, exasperated. What did I have to do to get laid on my birthday?

Livvie pulled away and righted her clothing.

"Don't be upset." She kissed me quickly before she scurried back into the kitchen to get her own breakfast. "You'll have plenty of time to play 'Kitten's been a naughty girl' later. I promise."

"We better," I grumbled. I picked up a piece of bacon and put it in my mouth. Rafiq wasn't what one would call a devout Muslim, but I was pretty sure he would roll over in his grave at the sight of me devouring bacon. I, for one, really enjoyed it in moderation. "So what do you have planned for me today? Please tell me it doesn't involve leaving the house."

Livvie glared at me ruefully.

"Don't be such a geezer, Sexy. Let's get out of here and have some fun."

"I *hate* fun."

Livvie laughed.

"You would. Good thing you'll never have to put out a personal ad." She assumed her ridiculous parody of my voice. "Hey, I'm James. I'm twenty-eight years old. I enjoy kicks to the face, having sex on kitchen counters, stalking my girlfriend, and telling kids to get off my lawn. I also hate fun. If you do too, hit me up." She was nearly doubled over while laughing at her own joke.

"I do *not* stalk you... anymore. Also, I've never yelled at anyone to get off our lawn."

"What about Claudia?"

"The front yard is not a place to tan." I couldn't help but laugh at the memory of turning the sprinklers on Claudia. She'd been mad as a hornet. I'd let her process her anger on the porch before Livvie let her back inside.

Livvie and I joked a lot over breakfast. Livvie is the only person I know who can make me furious one second and laugh the next. She likes to say I'm contrary, but I feel the same dichotomy is present in her. I suppose it keeps things interesting.

Livvie could not have planned a more perfect day. To begin, she assured me we would be spending the day alone. As much as I had come to like Claudia and Rubio, the only person I wanted to spend my first birthday with was Livvie. I never had to pretend with her. I could be myself—whoever that happened to be from one moment to the next.

Livvie was full of charm and whimsy. Since I'd missed out on so many birthdays, she was determined to show me what I'd missed. The first place she took me to was a go-kart racing track. Though small, the karts could reach speeds of up to forty-five miles an hour. Livvie won four out of seven races—she weighs less than me, so her car was inevitably faster. All things being equal, I'm sure I could have won every time. Of course, Livvie didn't quite see it that way. She is a very sore winner.

After go-karts, we ate pizza and played video games in the arcade upstairs. Livvie was no match for me when it came to shooting games, and I think we spent close to thirty Euros pumping change into a game called *Area 51*. If the earth is ever attacked by aliens, you're welcome to stand behind me.

By early evening, we were just finishing up eighteen holes of glow-in-the-dark mini golf. I was having one of the best days of my life and was spending it with the best person in my life. I couldn't wait to get Livvie home and express my gratitude to her for being everything I needed and far more than I deserved.

"You can't do that, Pet. You're cheating." I glared at Livvie as she picked up her ball and reset it on the mat.

"You distracted me. I should get to try again. It's the last hole." She stuck her tongue out.

"I distracted you while I was standing here being quiet?"

"Yes."

"I'll let you try again if you tell me you love me." I smiled my most wicked smile. The one I liked to give her just before I stripped her down and had my filthy way.

"You first," she said with a grin. She hit the ball and it rolled part way up the green before it failed to make it over the ice cream hill and rolled back toward her.

I laughed.

"That's what you get." Livvie kept hitting her ball until she made it into the hole. She was a sore winner and a very quiet loser.

"Are you hungry?" she asked as we were leaving.

"Not really. We've had a lot of junk." I hit the unlock button to the BMW.

"Well, just say you're hungry so I can suggest a place for dinner." She grinned.

"I'm starving!" I said.

"Me too! Luckily, I know of this new Italian place that opened up. We should go there."

I opened the door for Livvie and she gave me a kiss on the cheek before she got inside. I slid behind the wheel, and as I put the vehicle in gear to leave the parking lot, Livvie's hand was already on my thigh. She explained where to go while her fingers gently stroked me.

"Thank you, Kitten," I whispered.

"You're welcome, Sexy. Are you enjoying your birthday?"

"Immensely. I think tomorrow I'm going to try and find that arcade game." Retirement had opened me up to new hobbies. I discovered I really like video games.

"Men," Livvie scoffed. "You better not start ignoring me." She was pouting, but her heart wasn't in it.

"You're the one who encouraged me to get a PlayStation. I'm not the only bad influence in this vehicle." I casually put my hand on top of hers and held it the twenty minutes it took to get to the restaurant. When we arrived, I realized Livvie had lied to me about spending the entire day alone. Claudia and Rubio were already waiting to be seated. They held bags in their hands.

Claudia appeared giddy, and after hugging Livvie, she tossed herself at me.

"Happy birthday!" She planted a kiss on each of my cheeks. I begrudgingly returned the embrace and the kisses. Claudia is a good friend, and though I hate to admit it, I'd do most anything for her and Rubio.

Rubio shook my hand and wished me a happy birthday. He was wearing a pink shirt with grey pinstripes beneath a dark grey sweater and black slacks. It wasn't bad actually—for a moment he had me contemplating pink. Then I realized the shade matched the summer dress Claudia was wearing and I scrapped the idea. Livvie and I will never wear matching outfits. No!

"There is a fair in town. Claudia and I are going after dinner. You're welcome to come with us if you don't have other plans," Rubio said on the way to our table.

I looked ahead at Livvie, who was busy gabbing with Claudia about beating me at go-kart racing. She conveniently didn't supply the results of our shooting spree or mini-golf tournament. I smirked.

"We'll probably head home after dinner. I have one last gift waiting for me and I'm eager to open it."

Rubio blushed.

"I... yeah, ok." I nudged him with my shoulder and we laughed.

We ordered appetizers and salad since no one was particularly hungry. The restaurant was quaint and quiet. Most likely it was owned and operated by a single family. The food tasted homemade and was delicious. I almost wished I hadn't eaten so much pizza earlier, but it was difficult to regret any part of the day I'd had.

"Is it time for gifts? I'm so excited!" Claudia clapped her hands.

"I had to buy her that dress earlier. She always wants a present when someone else is getting one." Rubio laughed and kissed Claudia's bare shoulder. She didn't have the decency to look embarrassed and I found myself enjoying that aspect of her personality the best. With Claudia, what you saw was the truth. It's more than I could say about most.

"Do you want to open presents?" Livvie asked. She wriggled her eyebrows at me.

"I *suppose*." I feigned disinterest.

Claudia shoved her gift toward me first. It was a slender box and weighed practically nothing, but Claudia was nearly bursting with held laughter and excitement. I was instantly suspicious. Especially when she said to Livvie, "You have to make him wear it."

I tore away the paper and lifted the lid off of the box. I stared and stared and stared some more.

"What the hell *is* this?" I laughed. I shook the box and two plastic eyes wiggled around.

"Take it out," Livvie suggested. She had her hand over her mouth to hide her grin.

I obliged the group and regretted it. I had to smile though. It was funny and just the right touch of embarrassing. It was underwear.

"I assume I'm supposed to put my um… in the trunk of the elephant? Very clever. Rubio, do you also have a pair?" I tossed them onto his lap and he picked them up between thumb and forefinger. He slung them back at me.

"Sorry, friend. I don't do animal prints." We all laughed.

I received a new video game featuring the Mario Brothers from Rubio. I didn't know much about the game at the time, but let me assure you that many a day has been spent acquainting myself with the famous plumbers since.

"I'll be right back," Livvie said as she stood. "Claudia has my present for you. Open it." She kissed me and walked away before I could ask where she was going.

The box from Livvie was large and I ripped into it. I laughed hard when I saw the contents. Claudia was out of her seat and hovering over my shoulder. Rubio stayed in his seat but was trying to peer into the box. There was a piece of paper that read: Sexy's Kung-fu Boo-Boo Kit. Inside were rolls of bandages, band-aids, butterfly stiches, a bottle of peroxide, bath salts, a hand-made massage coupon entitling me to a "full body rub down (with happy ending)", and hand wraps "specifically designed for boxers."

I still had a smile on that could crack my face when the singing started. I looked up from my box and Livvie was walking toward me. The restaurant staff was carrying an entire tray of cupcakes with candles in them. They sang:

Happy birthday to you.

Happy birthday to you.
Happy birthday dear, James.
Happy birthday to you.

I stood up and reached for Livvie. She kissed me and whispered in my ear.

"One cupcake for every birthday, my love, and one more for good luck."

I couldn't stop staring at her as she pulled away. *I love you*, I wanted to say, but my throat felt closed and I was afraid of what would come out. There were tears in her eyes, and if I'd been a weaker man, there would have been tears in mine.

"What are you waiting for, the building to burn down?" Claudia chided. "Blow them out!"

I smiled, though I felt on the verge of falling apart. I kissed Livvie on her forehead and let my lips linger long enough for her to feel the depth of my appreciation. Then, for the first time I could remember, I blew out my birthday candles.

CHAPTER FIFTEEN

"Tell me how you feel." I ran the leather tongue of the riding crop along Livvie's outstretched arm. I watched as she shivered. The tiny hairs on her arm stood on end.

Livvie opened her mouth to speak, stopped, swallowed, and then replied.

"Excited," she said. She shivered again and the leather straps that held her in place on the cross creaked. There wouldn't be any kicking or flailing to interrupt me this time.

"Was that your first thought? I don't think it was." I continued down her arm and over her shoulder. I knew she liked it when I kissed her down her spine. I let the crop caress her where my lips typically would.

We hadn't done this before, not as lovers. I had my doubts about doing it at all, but she insisted. Her book was nearly finished. She'd been working on it more aggressively in the weeks leading up to her request. Between Livvie's writing, work, and school schedule, I'd hardly spent any time with her since my birthday. She needed this, she said. She needed to remember how it felt. She needed to recreate it.

I didn't want her to remember. *I* didn't want to remember. Yet, there I was, crop in hand. It was a pull too compelling to resist. I wouldn't use the belt. I wouldn't leave the marks I'd left the first time. If Livvie could re-imagine the events of our past, I could too. I could give her pain *and* pleasure. I could finally let the fading ghost of our past die and rest in peace. It was time for us to go on living.

I tapped her gently on her flank. She jumped.

"I asked you a question. Was excited your first response?"

"No," she whispered. "I'm... I'm afraid."

Yes, she was afraid. I'd learned her fear very well. In fact, I consider myself a connoisseur of fear. I know there are as many varieties of fear as there are colors in a rainbow. Livvie *was* afraid, but it was a brand of fear I very much enjoyed.

"Fear is part of it." I slapped at her inner thighs gently. I liked the sound it made. "You're defenseless. You're vulnerable. You're completely at my mercy." I stood behind her, unmoving, and I smelled her fear. True to her word, there was excitement as well. I leaned in and kissed the shell of her ear. "You. Are. *Mine*. Say it for me."

She sagged in her bonds. Her head fell on my shoulder and she nuzzled against me.

"I'm yours, Caleb." I was always Caleb while she was vulnerable. My name on her tongue reminded me of slipping into a worn pair of shoes. I'd been called Caleb most of my life, and were it not for Livvie, the name would be lost to me. Caleb had done horrible things—he'd been a monster—but he'd also allowed James to survive. Caleb deserved to live. I could be both men. I *am* both men.

I stepped back and took in the sight in front of me piece by piece. Her long mane of ebony hair cascaded down her slender back. I couldn't wait to hold it as I fucked her. I'd put her in red satin. Every miniscule movement caused the red fabric to shift and offer a different tantalizing bit of skin. The panties were scant. The meaty flesh of her backside appeared plumper by way of the cut. With her legs spread open on the X-shaped cross, I could catch glimpses of her pussy when she tried to adjust. Thick black straps made of leather held her in place at wrists and ankles.

My heart raced at the thought of whipping her. There was the hum of guilt living within me, but my baser urges banged like a drum in my veins. She was mine. She'd given herself to me, and I would take possession of her as surely as she had taken possession of my battered soul. The void in me had been filled by her love and forgiveness. All that she asked was that I give her all I had in me to give: my heart, my soul, my love, my secrets, my loyalty, and my whip hand.

I took her quickly and unaware across the bottom of her ass. Livvie's scream rent the air. James flinched at the sound, but Caleb's blood sang. I *am* both men.

Livvie's scream died just as suddenly as it had been born. Her lips were pressed together. Her hands were fisted above the leather straps holding her in place. A red stripe decorated her hindquarters.

"Tell me how you feel," I grated. I ran a hand along her quivering backside. I could already feel the welt.

"I…"Livvie croaked. "I don't know."

"Do you want me to continue?" I already knew the answer. I wanted her to know it too.

"Yes, Caleb." There was confidence in her voice.

"Anything for you, Pet." I did show mercy. I caressed her behind with my hand until I felt her muscles relax into my touch. "Let's start with more familiar ground." I raised my hand and slammed it forward. I hit one cheek first and then the other in rapid succession. I wanted her nice and warm before I used the crop again.

If Livvie could have moved, she'd have been up on her toes. I'd spanked her harder and not encountered quite so much movement, but it was my belief that restraints often invited slaves to thrash to their hearts' content. I had to remind myself Livvie had only ever played at the part of slave. She was mine of her own free will.

I stayed my hand from continuing to spank Livvie, but I did not keep it idle. Within seconds, my heated fingers wormed their way beneath the scrap of satin only just concealing her pussy. Her hips pushed back to meet me before she had a thought in her head. I liked that.

"Is that better, Pet? Did you like the spanking?"

She rocked her hips as much as she was able and tried to seat my fingers inside her.

"Yes, Caleb. Please, don't stop."

"I wouldn't dream of it." I pushed two fingers inside as far as they would go. I worked them back and forth quickly, delivering both jolts of pleasure and surprise. My dick jerked as Livvie's unabashed and lascivious yelp met my ears. I watched her hips move back and forth as she found her own pleasure. My sadistic appetite was slowly fed as, little by little, I withdrew my fingers and Livvie's hips gave chase to catch them. Back, back, back, she canted her hips as much as she was able. I hadn't given her much slack. She wouldn't have liked it if I had.

"More, Caleb. Please?" she whined. She treated me to the sight of her wiggling her bottom.

I spanked her once.

"Don't try to entice me. I'm not near finished with you. You wanted a whipping and I'm determined to give you one."

There was a sulky whimper preceding her murmured, "Yes, Caleb." She huffed and rearranged herself in her restraints.

"Always with the saucy mouth, Kitten. Whether you're using it to spout invective comments or simply petulant sounds, you're always pushing me toward this—toward punishing you. I always wondered—before—if you craved me like this. Did you?" I lifted the crop and let it land on her ass again. Livvie lurched in her bonds, her lips pressed tightly together so that not even her surprise could break free.

"Answer me, Kitten." I whipped her again and once more for good measure.

"No! No, Caleb." There was the slightest stirring of real fear in her voice.

"No? Why now? What's changed?" I whipped her again, mindful to keep the kiss of the crop across her flanks.

"I don't know," she cried. Her body was tight as a drawn bow. She was fighting me and I didn't know why. I thought perhaps she was only fighting herself.

"Do you remember the first time I whipped you?" I asked. I knew for certain she did. This entire scenario had been constructed based upon that particular memory. The least I could do was assist her in cataloging it properly.

"Yes, Caleb," she said more quickly.

"I remember too. It all could have gone differently." I reached around to the front of her body and cupped one of her breasts. I rolled her nipple between my fingers as I spoke. "I would have shown you mercy, of a sort. I knew you were scared. You'd been shocked to learn I was your abductor and not the hero you'd imagined." I tugged on her nipple. It was a hard little stone between my fingers. "You wouldn't let me be kind. I would have fed you while you rested your head in my lap. I would have given you as many answers as I could to ease your plight. You could have gone to bed without the marks from my belt. But you fought me. You couldn't win, and you still fought me."

"I hated you!" she said. The words caught in her throat. She shut her eyes and tears raced down her cheeks. "I didn't want your fucking mercy." The words were difficult to hear, but I knew them to be true and I deserved them.

I leaned forward and collected a salty tear from her cheek.

"Don't be sad, Kitten. You were right to hate me."

"I don't hate you anymore, Caleb. Please believe me. I don't hate you." More tears spilled down her cheek.

I stroked her hair. I kissed her salty cheek.

"I know, Pet. We've come a long way from there. Yet, here we are. You're still asking me to punish you. Why?" I struck her several times. With each loud slap her resolve crumbled a little more. I pushed her. I pushed myself. I wanted her to understand there had only ever been one reason to return to this.

Livvie was sobbing.

"I... I like it."

"Yes," I said. I placed my hand between her legs and stroked her wet folds. "You do. So why are you still fighting me?"

"I don't mean to!" Her chest shook with the force of her crying.

"I think you do. I think you believe I want you to— but I don't, Kitten. You don't have to provoke me. You're no longer my captive." I touched her clit. My fingertip glided easily through her slick folds. I whipped her across her other thigh with the crop.

Livvie screamed but settled quickly.

"I'm sorry, Caleb. Please forgive me."

Begging... I'm always a sucker for the begging when it suits my own desires.

"You're forgiven. Don't do it again."

She took several deep breaths.

"Yes, Caleb." She moaned loudly when I bit her shoulder. "God! The things you do to me..." Her breath shuddered from her chest. "No one else makes me feel this way. You hurt me so much—before. But you always made it better. You're the only one who makes it better. I don't want it to stop."

"Better than whom, Pet?" I dropped the crop and palmed her ass as I continued making circles on her clit. Livvie had found a taste for pain, but I knew the best way to get her to talk was to bring her as close to the edge of orgasm as possible.

"Everyone," she whispered. Her eyes were closed, but I could see the tears still leaking from her eyes. Her hips were moving again, finding a rhythm to match my touches. "You take care of me. No one's taken care of me like you."

A weight pressed on my chest.

"I'd take care of you without this."

"I want this. I didn't want it before. You didn't care about me. I was a thing to you. I know that's not true anymore. I trust you, Caleb. I trust you to see me like this. I trust you to take care of me." Livvie's thighs began to shake.

"No, Pet. You're not allowed to come yet."

"Please, Caleb," she whimpered.

I stifled a laugh.

"So manipulative." I spanked her with my bare hand. Hard. It didn't seem to affect her. She was on another plane.

"I learned from the best," she said. I watched her smile and then attempt to hide it.

"Couldn't make it five minutes, could you? And now I'm afraid I can't let you come."

"Caleb, no. *Please! I'm sorry.*" She opened her eyes when I pulled my hands away. Her expression was one of astonishment. I smiled.

"I warned you."

"What are you going to do?" Her tone suggested she was frightened. Her eyes said otherwise. She'd asked me that same question dozens, perhaps hundreds, of times. I always had the same answer.

"Whatever I want."

I'd been working on something rather special and I couldn't wait to try it out. I'd never been much of a carpenter or inventor, per se, but idle hands and an agile mind had led me to explore more hobbies. I found that I liked working with my hands, and I especially liked when my new hobbies coincided with my favorite pastime.

Livvie was silent as I undid the straps on her ankles. She was always most quiet when she was nervous. She sagged in my arms, limp as a wet noodle once I un-strapped her wrists.

"Caleb?" she whispered.

I hoisted her over my shoulder and slapped her ass.

"No questions, Pet. You'll like it. I promise. Or at the very least, *I will*."

I grabbed a pillow from the sofa before I walked the few steps necessary to reach my constructed apparatus. It hadn't taken much to put together. The downstairs was mostly unfinished and it was easy to find the choice support beams.

I tossed the pillow on the floor and set Livvie down on it. I heard her wince as her heated backside made contact, but I also knew she'd be just fine.

She appeared beautifully at odds with the unfinished basement, a diamond in the rubble.

"Lean back on your hands and put your legs out in front of you."

She stared at me for a moment as if she were unsure about whether or not to bait me with more of her insolent backtalk. Then, seeming to come to her senses, she did as I asked.

"Yes, Caleb," she added.

"Very good, Kitten. I'm proud of you." I winked at her and smiled. We were supposed to be having fun. I didn't want either of us to forget that fact.

"Thank you, Caleb." She managed a smile for me.

She was very curious about my every move as I gathered up the harness I needed, along with a spreader bar and some nylon rope. The hardware store was a very convenient place to shop for sex toys.

It took a few minutes, but I finally had what I wanted. Straps placed at Livvie's waist, thighs, and ankles would help lessen the amount of gravitational strain. The spreader bar would keep her ankles apart, evenly distribute her weight, and give her some semblance of balance. Finally, the nylon rope—anchored to the spreader bar and pulled through a series of load-bearing pulleys secured in the ceiling— would make it easy to lift her slowly off the ground.

"How do you feel?" I asked. Livvie lay on her back with her knees bent. She was pulling on her lip with her fingers.

"Nervous. Are you sure this is safe?"

"Do you trust me to keep you safe?" I palmed one of her breasts and traced her satin-clad nipple with my thumb. She sighed.

"Always."

"Then stop asking silly questions." I leaned down and kissed her. I was beyond aroused. I felt like a starving man sitting down to a feast. I wanted to touch every part of Livvie all at once. I also knew the wait would make the reward all the sweeter.

I let myself kiss her slowly. I let the tip of my tongue coax her lips open. I scraped it along the edge of her upper teeth before I felt the first slow slide of her tongue meeting mine.

Livvie's hand cupped the back of my head and pulled me closer. She was just as eager, but less inclined to savor than I was. Our teeth clicked against one another as she attempted to let the kiss consume us.

I pinched her nipple between my forefinger and thumb. I was treated to a keening whimper, a blatant request for more. I tugged Livvie's nipple, delivering sensation and rewarding myself with more of her whimpers.

"You really won't let me come?" she asked between kisses. One of her hands reached between my legs. She caressed my balls through my pants. Her fingernails dragged behind them. I shook.

"No."

"Please, Caleb." Her hand moved from my balls to my cock. She squeezed. "You're so hard. I know you want to fuck me."

A groan escaped me. I pulled away from her before she could convince me to let her have her way yet again.

"I do want to fuck you, Pet. I said *you* weren't allowed to come yet. I didn't say anything about not fucking you."

She frowned but kept from making further protests or demands. For Livvie, I supposed that qualified as being obedient.

Slowly, I pulled on the rope and hoisted Livvie into the air by her ankles. She gasped loudly and let out a yelp or two, but otherwise she'd come through it very well.

"Comfortable?" I asked. Anticipation burned hotly in my chest. I paid particular attention to the damp spot on Livvie's panties. I licked my lips.

"Um… I guess so." Her fingertips scrambled for purchase on the ground but couldn't quite reach.

"Relax your body and just hang there. The more you tense up, the more you'll move about." I secured the rope and grabbed a few items before I made my way to Livvie.

I ran my hands from her ankles down to her inner thighs. I stroked the little damp spot between Livvie's legs.

"Oh!" Livvie exclaimed. Her arms wrapped around my waist and she pulled me close. Her head was pressed against the front of my pants.

"My, but you *are* wet, Kitten. Did your whipping turn you on?"

"Yes, Caleb." She rubbed her face against my erection.

"I'm glad," I said. My voice was as hoarse as hers. I hooked my thumbs on either side of her panties and pulled them upward. They gave only as far as a few centimeters past the bottom of her ass. Her legs were spread too wide for much more. It was enough to suit my purpose.

"I've told you before, Kitten, but I'll say it again: You are beautiful here." I kissed her mound and Livvie's hips made a tiny thrust. "Should I lick your pussy?"

"Oh, god! Yes. Please." She began kissing my erection.

I palmed her ass in both hands and brought her to my mouth. I licked her from clit to delicious hole and darted my tongue inside to collect the wetness she'd so generously created for me. Livvie's entire body was shaking. Her hands gripped my ass and pulled me close.

"Mmm, I love the taste of your pussy. You should try it." I slowly backed away, ignoring whimpered protests. Placing one hand behind her neck and an arm behind her shoulders, I pulled Livvie upward and let her taste her pussy from my mouth.

She moaned and sucked on my tongue. Her hands held my head in place as she navigated her way through our upside down mashing of mouths.

"It's good, isn't it?"

"Yes, Caleb," she said through panting breaths.

Gingerly, I lowered her until our previous posture was achieved. I couldn't wait anymore. I wanted her mouth on me. I undid my slacks and pulled out my dick. Pre-come wept from the tip and I smeared it along Livvie's cheek.

Livvie turned her head and latched on to my cock like a vixen possessed. She suckled.

"Fuck!" I exclaimed. I couldn't stop myself from thrusting into her ravenous mouth. I reached for the back of her head and gathered up her hair from the floor. I held it in my fist as I let the first volleys of my lust clear. I had no intention of coming so soon. I pulled my cock out of her mouth with a wet pop.

"Easy, Pet. Let me set the pace. Open up." I wasn't at all surprised by her immediate obedience. With one hand holding her hair, I used my free hand to take hold of my cock. I couldn't resist tracing her wet, red lips with the tip of my cock. I sighed as I watched her kitten tongue dart out to lick it. Finally, I slipped back into the warm, suctioning sanctuary of her mouth.

I let go of Livvie's hair and stood. I desperately wanted more of her pussy in my mouth. I palmed her ass and pulled her toward me. My lips mouthed her clit while my tongue licked at her tiny bud. I felt every shudder, every moan, and every whimper against my cock. I made shallow thrusts interspersed with deep ones that drove past the scrape of Livvie's teeth into her throat.

I pulled my hips back every so often to allow Livvie to breathe. Drool coated her cheeks and puddled on the floor, but she'd never looked sexier to me.

"Tell me how you feel," I said.

She cleared her throat and swallowed.

"I want to come," she pleaded.

"No," I said. I urged her mouth back onto my cock. As she continued sucking, I bathed her pussy with my tongue until her thighs began to tremble. I pulled away. "No, Kitten." I ran my finger through her wetness and circled the tight pucker of her ass.

Her mouth pulled off my cock.

"I'll be good. I won't come. I won't come." She tried to wriggle away from my finger.

"Let me in. Now."

"*Please*, Caleb."

"I'll let you come." I pressed my lips to her clit and kissed her.

There was a moment of hesitation, and then I felt her muscles relax. I slipped the tip of my finger inside her ass and wiggled it back and forth.

"Oh, god! Caleb. Please! I'm going to die."

I laughed.

"You're not going to die, Pet. You're going to come. Hard."

"I want to." Her hips moved back and forth. "I'm so close. Please lick my pussy. I want to come. Please let me come."

"Put me back in your mouth."

The moment I felt her sucking, I put my mouth on her. I knew she couldn't take much more. *I* couldn't take much more, and I wasn't the one hanging upside down.

Livvie's hips thrust back and forth as she tried to work my tongue on her pussy. In the meantime, she was also fucking herself in the ass with my finger. A more glorious way to spend an evening has *not* been created.

I felt her muscles tightening. Even her mouth got tighter around my flesh.

"Go ahead and come for me, Pet." I cupped the back of her head and kept myself in her mouth as she came in mine. I felt her orgasm on my tongue, around my finger, and her cries of ecstasy vibrated along my cock. It felt as though she could come for days, and as I continued to fuck her mouth slowly my crisis found me and I spilled my seed inside.

Afterward, I lowered her to the ground and held her for a long time.

"Tell me again, Kitten." I kissed her forehead.

"I'm yours, Caleb. Always."

"And I'm yours. Happy anniversary, love."

"It was perfect," she whispered and nestled deeper into my arms.

I didn't have the energy to do much more than move us to the sofa. We slept for an hour or two before we could drag ourselves into the shower and then to bed where we made love again, soft and slow.

EPILOGUE

So, here we are at the end. Was it good for you? It was for me. I suppose in the end that's all that really matters. I know that's selfish, but you know I'm selfish and you love me anyway.

For what it's worth, I think I might actually miss you.

Will you miss me?

Will you cry?

If you do, please drink a tear for me and know that I never meant to cause you pain. Our parting is no cause to fret. In the words of Frank Herbert, *"There is no real ending. It's just the place where you stop the story."*

Livvie and I go on. We still live and have adventures.

Will we see each other again? I don't have the answer to that. Life has taught me to expect the unexpected and it's a lesson I learn over and again. Suffice to say – I hope so.

To be perfectly honest, I've gone around and around trying to find the perfect ending to this novel I never intended to write. In the end, I've come to the conclusion that there wasn't anything wrong with the way Livvie ended things. Her epilogue was short, but it captured the essence of our story: Survival is the most important thing. It affords us the chance to live and to find all of the things that make living worthwhile. I found redemption. I found forgiveness. I found love.

That said, Livvie did a beautiful job with the ending and I can think of no greater tribute than to end this book as she intended.

As I walked, I could feel his eyes on me, the way I could always feel his eyes on me. Tears ran down my face unabashed, but I didn't move to wipe them away. I had earned those tears, and I would wear them as a symbol of everything I had been through. They represented all the pain I had suffered, the love I felt, and the ocean of loss sweeping through my soul. I had finally learned to obey and never looked back.

The End
(For now)

About the Author

CJ Roberts is an independent writer. She favors dark and erotic stories with taboo twists. Her work has been called sexy and disturbing in the same sentence.

She also stalks her reviewers... What? Caleb had to come from somewhere!

She was born and raised in Southern California. Following high school, she joined the U.S. Air Force in 1998, served ten years and traveled the world.

She is married to an amazing and talented man who never stops impressing her; they have one beautiful daughter.

Stalk her on:
Facebook.com/AuthorCJRoberts
Twitter @AuthorCJRoberts
www.aboutcjroberts.com

56644277R00120

Made in the USA
Charleston, SC
25 May 2016